This book is a heartfelt tribute to the incredible staff at Teen Challenge Campuses worldwide, both past and present, and those who will join in the future. With special thanks to my 'then' leaders - 'now' friends: Ministers Scott and Barbara Stewart - four decades later and I still look up to you. Your unwavering support and guidance were a cornerstone in my journey. Your generous investment in me enabled me to advance from being a student to joining you serving as a staff member and began my journey of pouring into others' lives - for that, I am profoundly grateful. The knowledge and values you instilled in me, both as a student and as a staff, through your sacrifice and dedication, have prepared me for unforeseen challenges and opportunities. I am forever grateful and indebted to you.

Life Skills for Teens Made Simple

10 Rock-Solid Ways to Unleash Unshakable Confidence, Efficiently Manage Time and Money, Sharpen Your Cooking Prowess, and Much More for a Stress-Free Life

B. A. KNIGHT

© **Copyright 2024 - All rights reserved.**

The content contained within this book may not be reproduced, duplicated or transmitted without direct written permission from the author or the publisher.

Under no circumstances will any blame or legal responsibility be held against the publisher, or author, for any damages, reparation, or monetary loss due to the information contained within this book, either directly or indirectly.

Legal Notice:

This book is copyright protected. It is only for personal use. You cannot amend, distribute, sell, use, quote or paraphrase any part, or the content within this book, without the consent of the author or publisher.

Disclaimer Notice:

Please note the information contained within this document is for educational and entertainment purposes only. All effort has been executed to present accurate, up to date, reliable, complete information. No warranties of any kind are declared or implied. Readers acknowledge that the author is not engaged in the rendering of legal, financial, medical or professional advice. The content within this book has been derived from various sources. Please consult a licensed professional before attempting any techniques outlined in this book.

By reading this document, the reader agrees that under no circumstances is the author responsible for any losses, direct or indirect, that are incurred as a result of the use of the information contained within this document, including, but not limited to, errors, omissions, or inaccuracies.

ISBN: 978-1-963697-00-1

Table of Contents

INTRODUCTION 1

CHAPTER 1: COMMUNICATION SKILLS 5

    THE INTRICACIES OF EFFECTIVE COMMUNICATION 5
    VERBAL COMMUNICATION 6
    NONVERBAL COMMUNICATION 7
        Facial Expressions 9
        Eye Contact 10
        Use of Gestures 11
        Personal Space 12
    THE HEART OF COMMUNICATION: ACTIVE LISTENING AND EMPATHY 13
        Active Listening 13
        Empathy 16
    THE SIGNIFICANCE 18
        Navigating Social Challenges 19
        Academic and Professional Success 19
        Conflict Resolution 20
        Personal Development 20
        Preparing for the Future 21
    PUTTING IT ALL TOGETHER: MASTERING THE ART OF COMMUNICATION 21

CHAPTER 2. TIME MANAGEMENT 23

    BALANCING ACT: SCHOOL, EXTRACURRICULARS, AND A DASH OF "ME TIME" 23
        The Academic Arena: Mastering the Books and Your Extracurricular Activities 24
        The Sweet Spot: Navigating the Balance 25
    PRIORITIZATION: PICKING YOUR BATTLES 25
    THE ART OF SAYING NO 27
        How "No" Can Help 28
    WHY YOU NEED A SCHEDULE (YES, REALLY) 30
        Why Schedules Help: The Roadmap to Success 31
    HOW SCHEDULES WORK: A PRACTICAL EXAMPLE 32
    OTHER TIME MANAGEMENT TIPS 33

CHAPTER 3: EMOTIONAL INTELLIGENCE ... 37

UNDERSTANDING EMOTIONAL INTELLIGENCE ... 38
WHAT ARE EMOTIONS? ... 38
   Understanding and Managing Your Emotions ... 39
BUILDING EMOTIONAL RESILIENCE ... 45
   Acceptance of Change ... 46
   Developing a Growth Mindset and Supportive Relationships ... 47
COPING MECHANISMS FOR VARIOUS SITUATIONS ... 48

CHAPTER 4: GOAL SETTING AND PLANNING ... 53

WHAT IS A GOAL? ... 53
   Setting Clear Goals ... 54
   The Power of Goal Setting: An Eye-Opening Example ... 55
UNDERSTANDING SMART GOALS FOR TEENS ... 56
CREATING ACTION PLANS ... 59
   Strategic Thinking ... 59
   Breaking Down Goals into Objectives ... 59
   The Anatomy of an Action Plan ... 59
   Cultivating Habits for Success ... 60
BALANCING LONG-TERM VISION AND SHORT-TERM OBJECTIVES ... 60
   The Sweet Spot: Where Short-Term and Long-Term Meet ... 61

CHAPTER 5: THE BASICS OF PERSONAL FINANCE ... 63

WHY DOES PERSONAL FINANCE MATTER? ... 63
THE JOURNEY AHEAD: BASICS OF PERSONAL FINANCE ... 65
   Budgeting, Saving, and Spending Wisely ... 65
   Understanding Credit and Loans ... 71
FINANCIAL PLANNING FOR THE FUTURE ... 73
   Investing Wisely ... 73
SEEING PLANNING IN ACTION ... 74
   Why It Matters ... 75

CHAPTER 6: PROBLEM SOLVING AND CRITICAL THINKING ... 77

EMPOWERING DECISION-MAKING ... 77
   How to Make Empowered Decisions ... 79
NAVIGATING THE MAZE OF CHALLENGES ... 82
   How to Successfully Navigate Challenges in a Healthy Way ... 83
FUELING INNOVATION AND CREATIVITY ... 84
   How to Add Some Creative Spark ... 85
BUILDING RESILIENCE: TURNING SETBACKS INTO STEPPING STONES ... 86

How to Build Resilience *87*
THE JOURNEY AHEAD: PROBLEM SOLVING AND CRITICAL THINKING 88

CHAPTER 7: MAKING FRIENDS AND BUILDING RELATIONSHIPS 91

FRIENDS—WE NEED TO FIND THEM 92
   Why Trustworthy Friends Matter *93*
INITIATING CONVERSATIONS 94
   How to Begin *95*
FORMING MEANINGFUL CONNECTIONS 99

CHAPTER 8: HEALTH AND WELL-BEING 101

THE FOUNDATION OF PHYSICAL HEALTH 101
MENTAL WELL-BEING 103
FUELING THE BODY AND MIND: NOURISHING NUTRITION 104
BALANCING ACT: EFFECTIVE STRESS MANAGEMENT 106
   The Toll of Chronic Stress *107*

CHAPTER 9: ADAPTABILITY AND RESILIENCE 111

EMBRACING CHANGE 111
   The Multifaceted Importance of Adaptability *112*
   Fostering Adaptability Through Practical Techniques *113*
   Adaptability In Real-World Applications *114*
BUILDING RESILIENCE IN THE FACE OF ADVERSITY 116

CHAPTER 10: COOKING SKILLS 121

KITCHEN FUNDAMENTALS 121
   The Essential Knives: Your Kitchen Allies *121*
   Cutting Boards *124*
   Reliable Kitchen Tools *126*
MEASUREMENT MAGIC—COOKING MEASUREMENTS AND CONVERSIONS 128
   Teaspoons and Tablespoons *129*
   Measuring Cups *129*
   The Art of Effortlessly Converting Ingredients *130*
COOKING TECHNIQUES 131
   Boiling Basics *131*
   Sautéing *133*
   Baking *134*
   Exploring Different Food Prep Methods *136*
MEAL PLANNING AND NUTRITION 140
   Get Creative in the Kitchen *141*
   Meal Plan *142*

- Some Beginner Friendly Recipes 144
  - Grilled Chicken Salad 144
  - Grilled Lemon Herb Salmon with Braised Vegetables 145
  - Chocolate Chip Cookies 147
- Understanding Dietary Needs 149
  - Vegetarian Ventures 149
  - Protein Prowess 150
  - Flexible Eating 150
- Budget-Friendly Cooking 151
  - Smart Shopping Quest—Making Informed Grocery Choices 152

CONCLUSION 155

- Recap of Essential Life Skills 155
  - Encouragement for Continued Growth and Development 156

REFERENCES 159

Dear Reader,

As I extend my heartfelt thanks for choosing "Life Skills for Teens Made Simple," I want to express my profound gratitude. Your commitment to personal growth is truly inspiring.

To show my appreciation, I'm thrilled to present you with three invaluable gifts - assessments designed to illuminate your strengths and areas for growth. These assessments delve into crucial aspects of your development: communication skills, time management, and emotional intelligence.

Communication Skills Assessment: Understanding and honing effective communication is vital for you. This assessment will provide insights into your current communication style, enabling you to enhance your expression, active listening, and interpersonal skills.

Time Management Assessment: Time is a precious resource, and mastering its management is a lifelong skill. This assessment equips you with self-awareness, helping you identify your time utilization patterns to optimize productivity.

Emotional Intelligence Assessment: Navigating emotions is a key component of personal growth. This assessment helps you begin to recognize and understand your emotions and how emotional intelligence will serve you well in various aspects of life.

These assessments, coupled with "Life Skills for Teens Made Simple," create a comprehensive learning experience. They'll complement the book, providing actionable insights tailored to your unique journey.

Once again, thank you for being a part of this transformative journey. Your dedication to growth is not just inspiring—it's shaping the future of empowered individuals.

With gratitude,

B. A. KNIGHT

CLICK HERE:

Your 3 FREE Gifts await! CLICK HERE!

OR

SCAN THE QR CODE

Introduction

You're at the crossroads of your teenage years, facing a sea of dreams and responsibilities. It's a familiar scenario. We've all been there. The exams, the social whirlwind, and the whole adulting gig slowly creeping in—it's a lot to take in. But fear not because I've got a story for you that might hit home.

Meet Alex, a fellow teen navigating the maze of adolescence. Feeling overwhelmed by the whirlwind of exams and social events, Alex found a mentor that he could trust.

His mentor shared practical advice and personal experiences, making each obstacle a stepping stone instead of a wall to scale. Alex improved his communication skills with his mentor's encouragement, which helped him form even more meaningful connections with his friends. Together, they explored the intricacies of communication skills, turning conversations into meaningful connections.

So, why share this story? Because I hope you might find a mentor within the pages of this book. It's not just about facing these challenges alone; it's about having someone by your side, offering insights and support. Consider this your invitation to embark on this journey, guided by the words on a page and the wisdom shared in personal connections. Get ready for an adventure like no other!

Life Skills for Teens Made Simple goes beyond being just a guide—it's your lifeline tossed into the sea of uncertainties, handing you the tools to survive and thrive through the wild waves of adolescence.

Why are these skills so crucial for you? Well, it all boils down to the unique challenges and opportunities that make this part of your journey one for the books. More than any other age group, the line between dependence and independence is blurred. It's the time when the groundwork for your future is laid, and the habits you pick up become the sturdy pillars of your adult life. Exciting, right?

You may have wondered how to break through the barriers of communication that stifle your authentic voice. Maybe the ticking clock of deadlines and responsibilities keeps you awake at night, prompting questions about time management and the elusive balance between studies and self. Or, like many, you may find the landscape of relationships and emotional intelligence a perplexing puzzle.

Within these pages, we delve into the intricacies of these concerns and the practical solutions that can turn challenges into stepping stones toward personal growth. This book responds to the whispers of uncertainty, guiding you through the fog of doubts toward a brighter, more empowered future.

Join us on this quest through the life skills that transcend the traditional boundaries of education. Here's a glimpse of what awaits you:

- **Communication skills:** Learn to articulate your thoughts with the eloquence of a poet and connect with others on a profound level, forging friendships that will hopefully withstand the test of time.

- **Time management:** Be the architect of your schedule, creating a masterpiece that balances studies, social life, and personal passions while conquering the procrastination dragon.

- **Emotional intelligence:** Unlock the enigma of your emotions, honing the skill of empathy and fostering relationships that are not just surviving but thriving.

- **Goal setting and planning:** Transform nebulous dreams into tangible goals, and with a roadmap in hand, navigate the twists and turns toward your aspirations.

- **The basics of personal finance:** Navigate the labyrinth of money matters, from budgeting to investing, ensuring a stable financial foundation for your dreams.

- **Problem-solving and critical thinking:** Sharpen your analytical sword to cut through the thickest challenges, emerging victorious in adversity.

- **Making friends and building relationships:** Master the art of connection, creating a social network that enriches your life and lifts you to new heights.

- **Health and well-being:** Craft a sense of well-being where your body and mind are nurtured, ensuring you thrive in the demanding landscape of your teenage years.

- **Adaptability and resilience:** Develop the wings of resilience, soaring above setbacks and embracing change with the grace of a seasoned adventurer.

- **Cooking skills:** Enter the enchanting realm of the kitchen, where the alchemy of cooking becomes a source of joy, self-sufficiency, and shared moments with loved ones.

The journey ahead is unpredictable, but armed with these 10 life skills; you're not merely a passenger; you're the captain steering your own ship through the waves of adolescence, equipped to navigate the challenges and emerge victorious.

Chapter 1:

Communication Skills

Communication serves as the glue that unites us all. For a teenager navigating the terrain of self-discovery, effective communication lights your way through the maze of adolescence.

The Intricacies of Effective Communication

Effective communication goes beyond exchanging words; it's a dynamic and skillful engagement that plays a crucial role in various aspects of your life. As a teen, you will often grapple with complex thoughts and emotions; effective communication will allow you to express your ideas with clarity better, helping your peers, family, and educators understand you.

When you learn to communicate your feelings, you can foster better understanding and support. It encompasses the skill of expressing emotions constructively, be it sharing excitement, discussing fears, or conveying joy. Communicating your feelings fosters improved understanding of yourself and those around you.

In the classroom, effective communication helps you actively participate in class discussions, ask questions, and seek clarification whenever necessary. Whether giving a presentation or participating in group projects, solid communication skills can help you convey your thoughts persuasively, enhancing your academic performance. Learning those skills will help create a more positive learning environment.

As a teen, learning how to advocate for yourself is essential. Whether discussing your educational needs with your teachers, expressing your aspirations to your parents, or seeking guidance for personal growth, you must communicate effectively to get what you want. It enables you to seek advice, collaborate with others, and turn aspirations into actionable plans.

Effective communication becomes crucial for job interviews and professional interactions as you transition into adulthood. It involves presenting oneself confidently, showcasing skills, and articulating value.

Building a professional network requires effective communication. It is very important to master practical networking skills, which will help you to connect with mentors, peers, and professionals, opening doors for future opportunities.

Verbal Communication

As a teen, you're likely experiencing a surge of emotions and thoughts. It's crucial to take a moment before expressing yourself to consider the impact your words may have. Avoid derogatory language and choose words that convey your feelings and thoughts respectfully. Remember, your words are a reflection of your character.

In a world filled with distractions, actively listening to others is a skill that sets you apart. Put away your phone, make eye contact, and give your full attention to the speaker. Respond appropriately to show engagement—nod, ask follow-up questions, or offer affirming statements. By practicing active listening, you understand others better and build stronger connections.

Teenagers often find themselves amid information overload. When communicating, strive for clarity and brevity. Organize your thoughts before speaking, and get to the point without unnecessary details. This ensures that your message is understood and demonstrates respect for others' time and attention.

Don't be afraid to seek clarification or delve deeper into a topic by asking questions. Questions show curiosity and a desire to understand. Whether discussing school assignments, personal experiences, or world events, asking questions demonstrates your engagement and eagerness to learn.

Your tone of voice can convey more than the words you speak. Experiment with different tones to understand how they influence the perception of your message. A friendly and respectful tone promotes positive communication, while a harsh tone can create unnecessary tension. Be aware of your emotions and adjust your tone accordingly.

Nonverbal Communication

Your body language serves as a silent narrator that accompanies your spoken words. To project confidence, stand tall with an open posture and employ deliberate gestures that complement your speech. Pay attention to subtle movements; nodding can signal agreement, while crossed arms may indicate defensiveness. It is equally crucial to be attentive to the body language of others, as it offers valuable cues about their feelings and reactions.

- **Open posture:** Imagine you're giving a presentation in class. Standing tall with a relaxed posture—shoulders back, head held high—projects confidence. It suggests you are comfortable, knowledgeable, and ready to engage with your audience.

- **Gestures of agreement:** During a group discussion, you nod in agreement as a friend shares an exciting idea. This subtle movement communicates that you actively listen and support their perspective. It fosters a positive atmosphere and encourages further sharing.

- **Defensiveness posturing:** You cross your arms in a group conversation about a controversial topic. This defensive posture may signal discomfort or disagreement. Recognizing this cue helps you and others navigate the discussion with sensitivity and respect for differing opinions.

- **Observing others**: While discussing a sensitive topic with a friend, notice their body language. Are they leaning in with interest, or are they subtly pulling away? Understanding these cues allows you to gauge their comfort level and adjust the conversation accordingly.

- **Confidence in job interviews**: Picture yourself in a job interview. In addition to an open posture, maintaining a firm handshake and walking purposefully into the room conveys confidence. These nonverbal cues can leave a lasting positive impression on your potential employers.

- **Engagement in classroom discussions:** During a classroom discussion, leaning slightly forward in your chair and maintaining eye contact with the speaker demonstrates active participation. Combining this with nodding and gesturing subtly affirms your interest in the topic and encourages a dynamic exchange of ideas.

- **Mirroring body language:** When connecting with friends, pay attention to the subtle mirroring of body language. If your friend leans in, matching their posture fosters a sense of connection. This nonverbal synchronization can create a harmonious and comfortable atmosphere.

- **Avoidance of eye-rolling:** In a disagreement with a peer, refrain from rolling your eyes, as this can convey disrespect and dismissiveness. Instead, maintain a composed expression and express your differing opinions verbally, encouraging a constructive conversation.

Facial Expressions

Your face is a canvas of emotions. Learn to express yourself authentically through facial expressions. Smile when you're happy, furrow your brow when you're puzzled, and show empathy through your eyes. Understanding and interpreting the facial expressions of others helps you connect on a deeper level.

- **Expressing concern:** If a friend shares a personal challenge, a furrowed brow combined with a gentle head tilt can express genuine concern. This nonverbal cue communicates that you are emotionally invested in their well-being.

- **Surprise and excitement:** Imagine receiving an unexpected gift. Your widened eyes and raised eyebrows express surprise and excitement. Sharing these facial expressions with the gift giver enhances the moment's joy and strengthens your bond.

- **Frowning to communicate displeasure:** When someone crosses a personal boundary, a subtle frown

9

can signal displeasure without words. This nonverbal cue conveys your discomfort and sets clear boundaries in a non-confrontational manner.

- **Softening facial expressions during apologies:** When apologizing, soften your facial expressions to convey sincerity. A remorseful look, a lowered gaze, and a slight smile can help mend relationships by expressing genuine regret.

Eye Contact

Eyes are windows to the soul, and maintaining eye contact is a powerful form of nonverbal communication. It conveys sincerity, attentiveness, and confidence. Practice making eye contact without staring—strike a balance that makes others feel acknowledged and respected.

- **Expressing love and connection:** In personal relationships, prolonged eye contact during intimate moments expresses love and a deep emotional connection. This nonverbal gesture communicates a sense of vulnerability and trust.

- **Adjusting eye contact:** Distribute your eye contact evenly among participants during group conversations. This inclusive approach makes everyone feel valued and engaged. Adapt the duration and intensity of eye contact based on the context and the level of familiarity with each person.

- **Breaking eye contact to think:** While engaging in thoughtful conversation, it's acceptable to break eye contact briefly to gather your thoughts. Looking away momentarily can signal introspection rather than disinterest. Return your gaze with clarity once you're ready to continue.

Use of Gestures

Gestures can add flair and emphasis to your verbal communication. However, be aware of cultural differences in gesture interpretation. What might be innocuous in one culture could be offensive in another. Experiment with gestures that feel natural to you and align with the cultural context of your communication.

- **Expressing excitement with hand movements:** When sharing exciting news, accompany your words with enthusiastic hand movements. A raised fist, a thumbs-up, or a sweeping gesture can amplify the positive energy of your message, making it more engaging.

- **Navigating cross-cultural communication:** In a multicultural environment, attune to gesture norms. While a thumbs-up might signify approval in some cultures, it can be perceived differently in others. Adapting your gestures to align with cultural sensitivities fosters effective cross-cultural communication.

- **Using pointing for clarity:** During a presentation, judicious use of pointing can direct the audience's attention to specific points on a visual aid. This enhances clarity and helps your audience follow your narrative more effectively.

Personal Space

Respect personal space as a fundamental aspect of nonverbal communication. Different cultures and individuals have varying comfort zones regarding physical proximity. Pay attention to cues—if someone steps back, give them space. Being mindful of personal space demonstrates your respect for others' boundaries.

- **Respecting boundaries at social gatherings:** In a crowded social event, respecting personal space is crucial. Maintain a comfortable distance while engaging in conversation, allowing others to feel at ease in the lively atmosphere.

- **Consideration in collaborative work:** Be mindful of personal space during brainstorming sessions in collaborative projects. Providing enough physical room for everyone to contribute comfortably fosters a collaborative and creative environment.

- **Adapting to individual preferences:** Recognize that personal space preferences vary among individuals. Some people may appreciate closer proximity during conversations, while others prefer more distance. Respond to cues and adjust accordingly to ensure a respectful and comfortable interaction.

Understanding and applying these examples of nonverbal communication enrich your social interactions, making you a more perceptive and empathetic communicator. As you practice and refine these skills, you'll find that your ability to connect with others on a deeper level becomes an invaluable asset in various aspects of your life.

The Heart of Communication: Active Listening and Empathy

Communication is more than just words exchanged; it's about understanding and connecting with others on a deeper level.

Active Listening

Active listening is a crucial skill that involves fully engaging with the speaker, not just hearing the words but understanding the emotions and intentions behind them. It goes beyond passively receiving information; it's about showing genuine interest, respect, and a willingness to understand. Active listening is a valuable tool for building stronger connections, resolving conflicts, and navigating the challenges of adolescence.

Giving Them Your Full Attention

Active listening starts with being fully present. Put away distractions like your phone and focus on the person speaking. By giving your full attention, you understand the words, emotions, and nuances behind them.

- **Scenario:** Your friend is sharing a personal story about a challenging experience.
    - Put away your phone, turn off the TV, and make eye contact. Show that you are fully present and ready to listen.

Nonverbal Cues

Show that you're engaged in the conversation through verbal cues like nodding, saying "uh-huh," or offering brief affirmations. Nonverbal signals such as maintaining eye contact and open body language convey your attentiveness.

- **Scenario:** Your sibling is excitedly telling you about their day.
    - Nod your head, smile, and use enthusiastic facial expressions. These nonverbal cues show that you are engaged and interested in their story.

Ask Clarifying Questions

Don't hesitate to ask questions for clarification. This demonstrates your interest and ensures you understand the speaker's message accurately. It's a proactive way to prevent misunderstandings.

- **Scenario:** Your classmate is explaining a complex math problem.
    - Ask questions like, "Can you break that down a bit more?" or "I'm not sure I understand; can you give me an example?" Seeking clarification demonstrates your commitment to understanding the topic.

Reflective Responses

Reflect on what you've heard by summarizing or paraphrasing. This confirms your understanding and shows the speaker that their words are valued. For example, "So, what I'm hearing is…"

- **Scenario:** Your friend is expressing frustration about a group project.
    - Respond with, "It sounds like you're feeling overwhelmed with the project. Is that correct?" Summarizing their feelings shows that you're paying attention and trying to grasp the situation.

Avoid Interrupting

Patience is critical to active listening. Allow the speaker to express themselves fully without interruption. This creates a safe space for open communication and makes the speaker feel heard and respected.

- **Scenario:** Your parent is sharing their thoughts on a family matter.
    - Resist the urge to interrupt, even if you have a strong opinion. Let them express their thoughts thoroughly before offering your perspective. This demonstrates patience and respect.

Other Scenarios

- **Scenario:** Your friend is describing a disagreement with another friend.
    - Say something like, "If I understand correctly, you felt hurt because they didn't include you in the plans. Is that right?" Paraphrasing shows that you are actively trying to understand their point of view.

- **Scenario:** Your classmate is upset about receiving a low grade on a test.
    - Respond empathetically, saying, "I can imagine that getting a lower grade than expected is disappointing. How do you feel about it?" Acknowledge their emotions to show that you understand.
- **Scenario:** Your friend is sharing their aspirations for the future.
    - Use verbal cues like "That's amazing!" or "I believe in you." Positive verbal affirmations encourage them to share more and create a supportive atmosphere.

Empathy

Empathy, the ability to understand and share the feelings of others, is a powerful tool for fostering meaningful connections. This capacity enables you to comprehend the perspectives, experiences, and emotions of friends, family, and peers, forming the foundation of solid and supportive relationships.

When you demonstrate empathy, you create a safe space for others to express themselves authentically and foster trust and openness in relationships. This empathetic approach allows you to view conflicts from various angles, facilitating resolution and compromise in a positive and cooperative environment.

In group settings, empathy is essential for effective collaboration, as it helps you appreciate the strengths and challenges of your peers and contribute to a more harmonious and productive team dynamic. Additionally, empathy helps you respect and appreciate the diversity in your communities, encouraging an open-minded approach and reducing prejudice.

When you practice empathy, you are more likely to become a well-rounded individual. Empathy allows you to strengthen your interpersonal skills and help you genuinely connect with others on an emotional level. This empathetic quality complements active listening, enabling you to pick up on verbal and nonverbal cues, enhancing communication, reducing misunderstandings, and strengthening connections.

Moreover, empathy contributes to the development of emotional intelligence, making you more aware of your own emotions and those of others—a crucial aspect for personal growth and effective communication. This empathetic foundation allows you to be supportive friends during challenging times, offering comfort and reassurance.

Practical Steps for Practicing Empathy

- **Put yourself in their shoes:** Imagine what it feels like to be in someone else's situation, fostering a connection with their emotions and experiences.

- **Validate feelings:** Acknowledge and validate the emotions of the person you're communicating with, showing empathy and support.

- **Express understanding:** Let the person know you understand their feelings, demonstrating your ability to connect with their emotional state.

- **Be non-judgmental:** Maintain a non-judgmental mindset, creating a safe space for others to share their thoughts and feelings.

- **Show you care:** Being empathetic is more than just understanding; it's about having your friends' backs. When someone's going through a tough time, let them know you're there to lend a hand or simply to chat and offer support. You can say, "Hey, if you need anything or want to talk, I'm here for you." It's about being a friend who cares and is ready to help.

In essence, empathy is not only a cornerstone of positive social interaction but also a key element in personal growth. By practicing empathy, you can develop crucial life skills that create a more compassionate and understanding society, benefiting their relationships and individual journeys.

The Significance

Communication skills guide you through the maze of adolescence, helping you navigate relationships, understand yourself, and succeed in various aspects of life.

If you learn to master expressing yourself verbally, you can form deeper connections with peers, family, and mentors. You can then effectively articulate your thoughts, emotions, and ideas, fostering understanding and relationships.

Understanding and using nonverbal cues, such as body language and facial expressions, helps you convey sincerity, trustworthiness, and empathy. It adds depth to your communication, enhancing the quality of your relationships.

Navigating Social Challenges

Active listening is a lifeline in the tumultuous sea of teenage social interactions. It enables you to understand your peers, respond thoughtfully, and avoid misunderstandings. Active listening helps you to build trust and create a positive social environment by truly hearing others when they speak.

Empathy allows you to connect emotionally with your friends, family, and the world. It enables you to understand diverse perspectives, appreciate differences, and form friendships based on genuine understanding and support.

Academic and Professional Success

Mastering verbal communication is like becoming the artist of words—it's about letting your thoughts out and painting a vivid picture with your expressions. This skill isn't just handy in daily chit-chats; it's a game-changer in academic settings, where presenting ideas clearly can be the golden ticket to success.

Picture this: You're acing that class presentation, confidently articulating your thoughts, and making your ideas sparkle. When you can communicate effectively in the classroom, it's not just about getting good grades. It's about setting the stage for future triumphs in group projects and even paving the way for professional success.

But hold on. There's more to the communication mastery journey! As you gear up for the professional world, nonverbal communication steps into the spotlight. It's like adding a secret weapon to your arsenal. Knowing how to use gestures, maintain eye contact, and project the correct body language isn't just about looking cool (although that's a bonus); it's about creating positive impressions that leave a lasting mark.

Here's where empathy and active listening swoop in as the dynamic duo. Empathy is like the secret sauce that adds flavor to your words, making your communication clear and deeply understood. When you actively listen—tuning in, nodding along, and genuinely engaging with others—it's like turning on the charm in your communication dance. It's not just about talking; it's about creating a symphony where everyone's ideas are heard and appreciated.

So, whether you're rocking a class presentation, collaborating on a group project, or gearing up for future professional endeavors, remember, it's not just about what you say—it's about how you say it.

Conflict Resolution

Conflict is inevitable, but active listening gives you a powerful tool to navigate disagreements. It helps you understand the root of conflicts, find common ground, and work toward resolutions that benefit everyone involved.

Empathy is the antidote to hostility. If you practice empathy in conflict resolution, you create an atmosphere of understanding and compromise. This skill helps de-escalate tense situations, promoting healthier relationships.

Personal Development

Through active listening, you understand others and gain insights into their thoughts and emotions. It fosters self-reflection, contributing to personal growth and self-awareness.

Empathy is a cornerstone of emotional intelligence. When you cultivate empathy better, you begin to understand both yourself and others better, improving self-esteem, resilience, and overall emotional well-being.

Preparing for the Future

Mastering both verbal and nonverbal communication is a foundational skill for success in the adult world. It enhances job interviews, networking, and everyday interactions, setting the stage for future personal and professional achievements.

As you transition into adulthood, active listening and empathy become indispensable skills. Whether in personal relationships, workplaces, or community involvement, these skills contribute to effective collaboration, leadership, and community building.

Putting It All Together: Mastering the Art of Communication

Combining these verbal and nonverbal communication skills creates a harmonious and effective means of expressing yourself and understanding others. Remember, communication is dynamic, and mastering these skills takes practice. Be patient as you navigate the intricacies of verbal and nonverbal communication. As you develop these skills, you'll find that you're better equipped to navigate the challenges of adolescence, form meaningful connections, and lay the groundwork for future success in various aspects of your life.

The combination of active listening and empathy forms the heart of effective communication. When you actively listen, you show respect and understanding. When you empathize, you connect emotionally with others, creating a bond that transcends words.

This powerful duo fosters trust, strengthens relationships, and cultivates a positive and supportive communication environment.

As a teen navigating the complexities of adolescence, these skills will enhance your relationships and contribute to your growth as a compassionate and understanding individual. Practice active listening and empathy, and you'll discover their transformative impact on your connections with family, friends, and the world around you.

Chapter 2:

Time Management

Think of time management as your reliable companion, always by your side to help you navigate the challenges of your day. Instead of feeling overwhelmed, it empowers you to take charge and ensure that you allocate time for everything that truly matters.

As Dolin (2022, para. 10) points out, there are two types of kids when it comes to time management: Type 1, those with a loud internal clock who effortlessly navigate time and make adjustments as needed, and Type 2, those with a soft internal clock who struggle to be on time, meet deadlines, and plan effectively.

So, why invest in increasing your time management skills? These skills will help you ace exams and school projects and have plenty of free time left to pursue your interests outside of school. It's not just about making every hour count; it's about unlocking a future where you can chase your dreams and enjoy the things you love.

Balancing Act: School, Extracurriculars, and a Dash of "Me Time"

In the teenage hustle, where each day feels like a whirlwind of responsibilities and possibilities, finding the equilibrium between school, extracurriculars, and personal time is akin to mastering the art of spinning plates. Picture this: classes, club meetings, sports practices, perhaps a part-time gig to earn those extra bucks, and amid it all, a yearning for that precious "me time." It's a complex juggling act, but fear not, for time management is your trusty sidekick, the superhero cape that empowers you to soar through every challenge.

The Academic Arena: Mastering the Books and Your Extracurricular Activities

School often takes center stage. Classes, homework, exams—the academic realm demands attention and focus. It's not just about managing your time but understanding the ebb and flow of your energy. You need to prioritize your studies because your academic success is a cornerstone for your future.

Extracurricular activities add a splash of color to your routine. These engagements contribute to your personal growth, whether in sports, clubs, or community service. Balancing your schedule involves not just being physically present but mentally invested. Choose activities that align with your interests and long-term goals. Your time is precious, so spend it on pursuits that resonate with you.

Sports aren't just about physical fitness; they teach teamwork, resilience, and discipline. Balancing sports with academics requires strategic planning. Schedule practices, matches, and recovery time effectively. Recognize the symbiotic relationship between physical health and mental well-being, and watch as your prowess on the field complements your academic achievements.

"Me Time:" A Sanctuary in the Chaos

Appreciating your social connections is crucial in the academic and extracurricular hustle. Friends and hangouts contribute to your emotional well-being. Allocate time for these moments; they're not just leisure but essential for maintaining a healthy balance. The art lies in being present during these interactions, genuinely enjoying the company of friends without the looming shadow of pending tasks.

Personal time is not a luxury; it's a necessity. In this balancing act, carve out moments exclusively for yourself. Whether reading a book, listening to music, or simply staring at the clouds, these pockets of solitude rejuvenate your spirit. They're not a guilty pleasure but a crucial element in the grand tapestry of your well-being.

The Sweet Spot: Navigating the Balance

Finding the sweet balance isn't a one-size-fits-all equation. It's a dynamic process of trial and error. Tweak your schedule, learn from experiences, and adapt to the evolving demands of each plate you're spinning. Remember, it's not about perfection but about cultivating a harmonious blend of academics, extracurriculars, and personal time—a chorus that resonates with the rhythm of your life.

Prioritization: Picking Your Battles

Imagine a warrior stepping onto the battlefield, strategically choosing where to strike instead of attempting to conquer every inch. That's the essence of proper time prioritization—a secret weapon and a compass in the wilderness of tasks.

Have you ever felt like drowning in a sea of assignments, chores, and commitments? Prioritization is your lifeguard, helping you stay afloat by focusing on what truly matters. It's not just about managing time; it's about investing it where it counts.

In the words of Eisenhower (2011, para. 1), the "Urgent-Important Matrix helps you decide on and prioritize tasks by urgency and importance, sorting out less urgent and important tasks which you should either delegate or not do at all." Prioritizing tasks by urgency and importance leads to four quadrants with different work strategies: do first, schedule, delegate, and don't do (Eisenhower, 2011, para. 4).

Picture a grid divided into urgent, important, less important, and neither critical nor essential. Your goal? Tackle tasks in the urgent-important quadrant first, then move outward. As your strategic ally, the Eisenhower Matrix helps you prioritize tasks, ensuring that your actions align with your goals.

Consider your energy cycles. Are you a morning person? Reserve your peak hours for high-priority tasks. As Vaccaro (2000) suggests, the Pareto Principle indicates that roughly 80% of effects come from 20% of causes. Identify the vital 20% and focus on them for maximum impact.

The 80/20 rule, according to Vaccaro (2000, para. 3), states that the relationship between input and output is rarely balanced. When applied to work, approximately 20% of your efforts produce 80% of the results. Recognizing and focusing on that 20% is the key to making the most effective use of your time.

Remember, life isn't about conquering everything; it's about focusing on the right things. Prioritization isn't a one-time thing; it's a mindset. Be strategic and intentional, and recognize that you can't do everything but can do what truly matters.

The Art of Saying No

Sometimes, the most potent weapon in your arsenal is the ability to say no. It's not about avoiding challenges but preserving your energy for the battles that align with your goals.

The word *no* often carries a negative connotation. However, when wielded with intention and purpose, it transforms into your most potent shield, guarding you against unnecessary commitments and distractions.

Saying no is not a declaration of weakness; it's a proclamation of self-awareness and resilience. Think of it as your shield against the arrows of overcommitment and burnout. You're not dismissing opportunities by uttering that two-letter word; you're carefully curating your battlefield to ensure victory in the right conflicts.

Imagine your energy as a finite resource, akin to a superhero's power. Every time you say yes to something, you're expending a portion of that power. Saying no isn't laziness or reluctance; it's about conserving your energy for the battles that truly matter and align with your overarching mission.

Not every battle is worth fighting, and not every invitation deserves a yes. The strategic no involves evaluating the request or opportunity in the context of your goals and values. Does it propel you toward your objectives or divert you down a side quest? Your time and energy are precious, so spend them on endeavors that contribute meaningfully to your journey.

Saying no is also about establishing and maintaining healthy boundaries. It's about recognizing the limits of your time and capacity, and it's a crucial act of self-care. Just as a knight wouldn't charge into battle without proper armor, you shouldn't dive into commitments without considering the toll they may take on your well-being.

Crafting a no requires finesse. Instead of a blunt rejection, consider expressing your appreciation for the opportunity and explaining your current commitments or priorities. This transforms a simple denial into a diplomatic declaration, showcasing your respect for the other party while prioritizing your goals.

In time management, you say no, which grants you the freedom to dictate your narrative. It's about taking charge of your schedule rather than being a slave. The more you exercise this freedom, the more you align your actions with your aspirations.

The art of saying no isn't a skill reserved for the aloof or the uninterested. It's a strategic move, a powerful weapon in your arsenal, allowing you to preserve your energy for the battles that align with your goals. Embrace it, wield it wisely, and watch as the battles you choose to fight become the defining moments of your journey.

How "No" Can Help

Meet Jake, a high school senior with big dreams of passing his exams, playing varsity soccer, and conquering the world of coding. Jake was the go-to guy in his class—always willing to lend a hand, accept every invitation, and tackle any challenge that came his way. His eagerness to please made him the hero of the moment, but little did he know his time management skills would be tested.

One day, Jake found himself knee-deep in a coding project that demanded intense focus and dedication. Simultaneously, the school soccer season kicked into high gear with rigorous training sessions and weekend matches. On top of that, his friends were organizing a charity event, and Jake, being the reliable guy he was, couldn't say no to lending a hand.

Weeks passed, and the once-promising coding project started lagging. Jake found himself burnt out, sleep-deprived, and struggling to maintain his grades. His once-spotless schedule turned into a chaotic battleground, and he was losing the war against time.

One evening, as he stared at his unfinished code and a mountain of textbooks, Jake had an epiphany. It wasn't that he lacked dedication or skills; his inability to say no led him down this exhausting path.

With a newfound understanding, Jake began to assess his commitments. Soccer, coding, and charity work were all significant battles, but he needed to prioritize. Hesitant but determined, Jake approached his friends and explained his situation. He gracefully declined additional responsibilities for the charity event, freeing up precious hours for coding and much-needed downtime.

The immediate relief was palpable. Suddenly, Jake had the time and mental bandwidth to truly focus on his coding project. The soccer field became a place of enjoyment rather than stress, and he discovered that saying no didn't make him any less of a team player.

Ultimately, Jake's coding project met the deadline and exceeded expectations. His soccer performance improved; he even had time for self-care and relaxation. Jake learned that saying no wasn't a rejection of opportunities but a strategic move to preserve his energy for the battles that truly mattered. His journey from being overwhelmed to being in control became a testament to the transformative power of mastering the art of saying no and prioritizing battles wisely.

Why You Need a Schedule (Yes, Really)

Schedules, often viewed as the strict rules of adulthood, take on a new role during the whirlwind of adolescence, becoming a secret weapon—a roadmap to success. While the spontaneity of teen life may be tempting, a well-crafted schedule is a reliable guide, ensuring you navigate the chaos without missing out on the good stuff.

According to Dolin (2022, para. 22), struggles with time management can be linked to weak executive functioning skills, which involve regulating emotions and reasoning. Without a schedule, dealing with school assignments, extracurricular commitments, social obligations, and personal passions is like embarking on a cross-country road trip without a map—you might stumble upon exciting places, but reaching your destination becomes a shot in the dark.

To gauge if your child might face challenges with weak executive functioning skills, Dolin (2022, para. 23) suggests considering factors such as difficulty getting started, sustaining effort, inhibiting distractions, and shifting between tasks.

Dr. Timothy Pychyl, a procrastination researcher, as cited by Dolin (2022, para. 34), emphasizes that emotion is at the core of procrastination. The challenge arises when individuals feel the need to be in a good mood to tackle an uninteresting task, leading them to opt for more pleasurable activities instead of addressing the task at hand (Dolin, 2022, para. 35).

Think of your schedule as the GPS of your daily journey—it doesn't restrict your freedom but provides a structured path to reach your desired destinations efficiently. Without it, you might be caught amid urgent tasks, neglecting activities that truly matter.

The beauty of a schedule lies in its ability to carve out dedicated moments for joy, growth, and fulfillment. Instead of succumbing to the tyranny of the urgent, a well-crafted schedule empowers you to proactively allocate time for activities that contribute to your overall well-being.

Have you ever felt overwhelmed by the sheer volume of tasks? A schedule acts as a filter, helping you identify priorities and allocate time based on their importance. It transforms the chaotic barrage of responsibilities into a manageable sequence, allowing you to approach each task with focus and efficiency.

Without a schedule, you might be in a perpetual state of reaction—responding to the urgent rather than proactively shaping your day. A plan empowers you to be the architect of your time, making intentional choices about how you spend each precious moment.

Contrary to popular belief, schedules aren't about rigidity. They offer a structured framework within which you can adapt and accommodate changes. Think of it as a well-choreographed dance—there's a rhythm, but there's room for improvisation.

Why Schedules Help: The Roadmap to Success

- **Efficient time allocation:** Imagine having a buffet of your favorite foods, but you only have a limited plate size. A schedule helps you pick and choose what to put on your plate—allocating time efficiently based on priorities. This prevents you from overloading on the less important and ensures you savor every bite of what truly matters.

- **Prioritization made easy:** Life bombards you with a constant stream of tasks, each claiming urgency. A schedule acts as your shield, helping you identify and prioritize tasks based on importance. The superhero cape allows you to tackle challenges methodically, ensuring you conquer the significant battles first.

- **Balancing act:** Much like a tightrope walker with a balancing pole, a schedule aids in maintaining equilibrium. It prevents you from leaning too much into one area of your life, academics, extracurriculars, or personal time. The result? It is a well-rounded, fulfilling experience.

- **Reducing decision fatigue:** Have you ever stood in front of an open fridge, unable to decide what to eat? Decision fatigue is accurate, and schedules act as decision-making anchors. They eliminate the dilemma of choosing what to do next, allowing your mind to focus on the tasks rather than getting lost in the labyrinth of choices.

How Schedules Work: A Practical Example

Let's meet Sarah, a high school junior with dreams of passing her exams, excelling in debate club, and still having time for her art. Without a schedule, her days became a chaotic mishmash of schoolwork, club meetings, and spontaneous hangouts.

With a schedule, Sarah could allocate specific time blocks for each activity. She dedicated mornings to focused study sessions, afternoons to debate club and other extracurriculars, and evenings to pursue her artistic passions. Weekends were strategically reserved for downtime, allowing her the freedom to relax and recharge.

The result? Sarah aced her exams and became a standout member of the debate club. Her art flourished, and she found time for meaningful social interactions. The schedule wasn't a restrictive set of rules; it was her ally, enabling her to navigate the labyrinth of high school life with purpose and efficiency.

So, why do you need a schedule? Because it's not just a piece of paper filled with time slots; it's your personalized compass, guiding you through the chaos of teenage life. It's the key to unlocking efficiency, productivity, and, most importantly, the ability to make time for the good stuff that makes your journey truly memorable. Embrace the power of scheduling, and watch as your days transform into a harmonious symphony of productivity and joy.

Other Time Management Tips

Have you ever heard of the Pomodoro Technique? It's not just a fancy timer; think of it as your brain's superhero. Break your tasks into 25-minute focused chunks called "Pomodoros," then take a chill 5-minute break. After 4 Pomodoros, treat yourself to a longer break (15-30 minutes). It's like saving the day from burnout while keeping your productivity high!

Imagine your day as a canvas waiting for your energy masterpieces. Time blocking is like using an artist's brush—you categorize your day into cool themes. Mornings are for serious work, afternoons are for meetings or classes, and evenings are for chilling or doing your thing. It turns your day into a chill symphony of excellent activities.

Okay, some are just tiny ripples in the sea of tasks. That's where the two-minute rule comes in. If something takes less than two minutes, tackle it right away. No letting tiny tasks pile up into a massive wave of stress!

Your digital gadgets can be your sidekicks, not distractions. Use apps like Trello, Todoist, or Asana to sort your tasks. Set reminders on your phone or computer—turn them into your superhero helpers that sync up with your plans.

Guess what? Delegating tasks isn't a sign of weakness; it's like being a strategy genius. Find stuff others can handle well and let them shine. It frees up your time for the missions that match your strengths and goals.

Your time management strategy is like a living thing, changing every day. Take some time to think about what's working and what could be even cooler. Being flexible is your superpower in handling the ups and downs of your schedule.

Have you ever tried mindful time-tracking? It's like shining a light on your day. See what you're doing, where you could improve, and tweak things. Being aware helps you use your time like a pro.

Now, your ambitions–they're not towering mountains; they're more like climbable hills. Break big tasks into smaller, doable goals. It makes reaching the top less scary and way more satisfying.

These time management tricks are like your secret weapons. Try them out, see what clicks, and watch how your day transforms. Experiment, be flexible, and soon you'll be the master of your time!

Oh, and a bonus tip: Plan your week on Sundays. It's like having a map so Monday doesn't hit you like a ton of bricks. Group similar tasks together during your day to keep your flow going. Know your limits, and be realistic about what you can do. Time management is a skill you'll get better at with practice. Find what works for you, adjust as things change, and rock that balance between school, activities, and your chill time.

Chapter 3:

Emotional Intelligence

Imagine this: you're in the middle of a bustling school day, facing a challenging assignment, when suddenly, frustration creeps in like an unwelcome guest. Instead of succumbing to the pressure, you take a deep breath, identify the disappointment, and channel it into a focused burst of energy. The result? This brilliantly executed project showcases your academic prowess and reveals your ability to master your emotions.

This scenario encapsulates the essence of emotional intelligence, a skill set that empowers you to navigate the twists and turns of your emotional landscape with finesse. It's not about suppressing emotions or pretending they don't exist—it's about understanding them, leveraging their power, and steering them in a direction that propels you toward success.

Soon, you will see how important it is to travel deep into the heart of your emotions, uncover the mysteries of self-awareness, and equip you with the tools to forge stronger connections with others. You'll discover that emotional intelligence isn't just a buzzword; it's a dynamic force that can shape the course of your relationships, academic endeavors, and personal growth.

So, buckle up and get ready to tap into your emotional potential. You'll find that the ability to understand and manage your emotions isn't just a skill—it's your passport to a more resilient, empowered, and fulfilling life.

Understanding Emotional Intelligence

Emotional intelligence is a vital skill that empowers individuals to recognize, understand, and manage their emotions and those of others. It involves perceiving emotions, reasoning with emotions, understanding emotions, and managing emotions effectively. It's about awareness of your feelings, constructively navigating them, and empathizing with others.

What Are Emotions?

Emotions are complex reactions to stimuli that involve physiological changes, expressive behaviors, and subjective experiences. They are a fundamental part of being human, ranging from joy and excitement to anger and sadness. Understanding emotions is the first step in developing emotional intelligence.

You are in an intense self-discovery and identity-formation phase as a teen. Recognizing and understanding your emotions helps you know your values, desires, and preferences. This self-awareness forms the foundation for building a solid and authentic sense of self.

During adolescence, social dynamics become more complex, and peer relationships are central. Understanding emotions enables navigating social situations, empathizing with others, and building healthier connections. It fosters effective communication and reduces the likelihood of conflicts.

Emotional well-being is closely linked to cognitive functioning. When you recognize and manage your emotions, you are better equipped to handle stress, focus on tasks, and make informed decisions. This positively impacts your academic performance and overall learning experience.

As a teen, you will face various stressors, including academic pressures, social challenges, and changes in family dynamics. Emotional intelligence equips you with coping mechanisms to navigate these stressors, fostering resilience and adaptability in adversity.

The teenage years are a critical period for mental health development. Understanding emotions helps you identify signs of emotional distress, seek appropriate support, and engage in self-care. It promotes a proactive approach to mental well-being, reducing the stigma of seeking help.

Emotional intelligence plays a significant role in decision-making. When you can assess their emotions and consider the feelings of others, you are more likely to make thoughtful, responsible choices. This is particularly important as you navigate decisions related to academics, relationships, and plans.

As a teen, you will often experience intense emotions, and learning to regulate these emotions is critical to your well-being. Understanding how to manage stress, anxiety, and anger contributes to a more balanced emotional state and prevents impulsive or harmful behavior.

Understanding and Managing Your Emotions

Taking the time to identify and name your emotions is like unlocking a treasure chest of self-awareness. Imagine navigating the maze of your feelings—pause momentarily, observe your feelings, and put a name to it. Are you experiencing excitement, frustration, joy, or maybe a mix of emotions? This self-awareness is your guide through the maze of your inner world.

Navigating this emotional maze can seem daunting at first. Fear not—the most critical step in the maze is easy. It begins with learning how to identify and name your emotions.

Start by carving out a few moments in your day to think about your emotions. It could be during your morning routine, a quiet moment before bed, or even a quick moment during a hectic day. Close your eyes, take a deep breath, and let your mind settle. Now, observe. What emotions are swirling within you? Is there a subtle hum of excitement, a tinge of frustration, a burst of joy, or perhaps a complex mix of feelings? Allow yourself the space to be aware simply.

Keeping an emotion journal is another way to examine your emotions. Divide it into sections for all emotions, and regularly jot down your feelings. Be specific—instead of labeling it as *happy*, explore whether it's pure joy, contentment, or a touch of gratitude. Over time, patterns might give you some insight into how you feel.

Initially, setting reminders on your phone to check in with your emotions throughout the day is a good idea. During these check-ins, ask yourself how you're feeling and why. It's a practice that keeps you connected to the ebb and flow of your emotional tide.

Sometimes, verbalizing your emotions brings about a better sense of understanding. Try to have open conversations about your feelings with friends and family. When you share your emotional experiences, you strengthen your connection to others and also help you better understand your emotions.

Imagine these practices as tools in your emotional toolkit—a set of keys that unlock the doors to self-awareness, creative expression, and inner peace. Remember that understanding your emotions is continuous exploration. Your feelings are just like yours; they change and evolve.

Express Yourself

Once you've acknowledged your emotions, the subsequent step is to give them a voice. Seek out creative and healthy outlets to express what's inside, envisioning your feelings as colors waiting to be painted on a canvas, whether through art, journal writing, or engaging in a heart-to-heart conversation with a trusted friend; expressing your feelings is a transformative act, akin to releasing a kite into the open sky—allowing your emotions to soar freely.

As emphasized by Sosnoski (2021, para. 28), "Self-expression is not manipulative, controlling, or a bid for popularity." Honest self-expression is a bold and brave act, and learning how to express yourself may take some time. Especially when feeling vulnerable with others, it helps to remember the benefits (Sosnoski, 2021, para. 32).

- **Artistic outlets**
    - **Visual arts:** Explore drawing, painting, or sculpting. Let your emotions guide your creative process. For example, if you're feeling joy, use bright and vibrant colors; if it's sadness, perhaps use softer tones.
    - **Photography:** Capture moments that reflect your emotions. Compile a visual diary that tells the story of your feelings through images.
- **Creative writing**
    - **Journaling:** Pour your emotions onto the pages of a journal—write freely without judgment. Describe what you're feeling, why, and any insights gained. It's like having a private conversation with yourself.

- - **Poetry or songwriting:** Turn your emotions into verses or lyrics. Expressing feelings through rhythm and rhyme can be both cathartic and empowering.

- **Conversations and communication**

  - **Heart-to-heart talks:** Reach out to a trusted friend, family member, or mentor. Share your feelings openly and actively listen to their perspective. Sometimes, articulating emotions out loud helps you gain clarity.

  - **Expressive communication:** Use "I" statements to express your emotions assertively. For example, say, "I feel excited about this project because..." This helps you communicate your feelings without placing blame.

- **Physical outlets**

  - **Dance or movement:** Allow your body to express what words can't. Move freely, letting the rhythm guide your movements. This is a powerful way to release pent-up energy and emotions.

  - **Exercise:** Engage in physical activities. Exercise releases endorphins, the body's natural mood lifters.

- **Create a feelings collage**

  - **Magazine cutouts:** Collect images and words from magazines that resonate with your emotions. Create a collage that visually represents your current emotional state.

- **Join creative communities**
    - **Art or writing groups:** Join clubs or online communities where you can share your creative expressions with like-minded individuals.

Remember, expressing your emotions is not about creating a masterpiece but the process and the release it brings. Just as a kite soars freely when released, your feelings gain freedom and perspective when expressed healthily. Experiment with different outlets, find what resonates with you, and allow your emotional landscape to flourish.

Reflect on Triggers

Emotions, much like the branches of a tree, extend deep into the soil of our experiences and perceptions. To truly understand the nuances of your emotional landscape, it's essential to embark on a journey of reflection—specifically, reflecting on the triggers that set these dynamic processes in motion. Think of it as navigating through the undergrowth of your mind, armed with the flashlight of introspection.

- **Journaling your experiences:** Begin by keeping a reflective journal. After moments of heightened emotion, jot down the details of the situation. What happened? Who was involved? How did you feel? His process serves as a compass, guiding you back to the origin of your emotions.

- **Identify patterns**: As you journal your experiences, look for patterns or recurring themes. Are there specific situations or people that consistently evoke similar emotional responses? Patterns are like signposts pointing you toward the underlying causes of your feelings.

- **Explore childhood experiences:** Our early experiences often shape our emotional responses. Reflect on your childhood and upbringing. Are there events or dynamics that may influence how you react to certain situations? Understanding these connections provides valuable context.

- **Trigger awareness exercise:** Engage in a trigger awareness exercise. When you feel a strong emotion, pause and ask yourself: What triggered this response? Is it a person, a place, or a specific circumstance?

- **Seek feedback from others:** Sometimes, those close to us can offer valuable insights. Ask friends or family for feedback on your emotional responses.

- **Therapeutic support:** If certain emotions or triggers prove challenging to unravel, seeking the guidance of a mental health professional can be immensely beneficial. Therapists are skilled at helping individuals explore and understand the roots of their emotions.

- **Challenge distorted thinking:** Reflect on whether specific thought patterns contribute to emotional triggers. Are there cognitive distortions at play, such as catastrophizing or overgeneralization? Challenging and reframing these thoughts can alter your emotional responses.

- **Reflect on past resolutions:** Recall instances when you successfully managed or resolved challenging emotions. What strategies did you employ? Reflecting on past successes provides a roadmap for navigating similar triggers in the future.

Understanding your emotional triggers is akin to being an archaeologist, excavating layers to reveal hidden artifacts. By shining a light on the root causes of your emotions, you gain mastery over your responses, transforming triggers from stumbling blocks into stepping stones.

Building Emotional Resilience

As a teen, you are at a pivotal point in your life. Your choices are laying the groundwork for emotional resilience—the invaluable capacity to rebound from challenges and confront the intricacies of adolescence with strength and adaptability. As you become more aware of your emotions, you also become more resilient.

In the words of Chowdhury (2019, para. 9), "Emotional resilience means bouncing back from a stressful encounter and not letting it affect our internal motivation. It is not a 'bend but doesn't break' trait; resilience is accepting that 'I am broken' and continuing to grow with the broken pieces together."

Recognizing and Accepting Emotions

Embarking on the journey of understanding and managing your emotions starts with a crucial first step—learning to recognize and wholeheartedly embrace what you're feeling. This initial skill lays the foundation for navigating life's challenges with a deeper self-awareness.

Take a moment to acknowledge and welcome your emotions intentionally. This process involves identifying what you're feeling and comprehending the complexity of those emotions. It's about pausing to reflect on the ebb and flow of your inner experiences.

As you navigate this emotional journey, remember that it's more than just acknowledging the existence of emotions; it's about developing emotional intelligence. This means going beyond surface-level recognition to understand each emotion's nuances truly. Whether joy, sadness, excitement, or frustration, each emotion has its own story.

The path forward includes actively processing these emotions. Instead of bottling or letting them simmer beneath the surface, engage in a reflective practice. Consider journaling your thoughts, talking to a trusted friend, or engaging in creative activities that allow you to express and make sense of your feelings.

In embracing the idea that emotions are an integral part of the human experience, you're not just acknowledging their existence; you're validating their significance in shaping who you are. This acceptance contributes to the growth of emotional intelligence—an invaluable tool for navigating the complexities of life.

So, as you travel through your journey's ups and downs, remember that embracing your emotions is not a sign of weakness but a testament to your authenticity. It's a conscious choice to live a life marked by self-awareness, resilience, and a positive outlook, knowing that your emotions are an essential and legitimate aspect of your unique path.

Acceptance of Change

A fundamental pillar of building emotional resilience involves wholeheartedly accepting the unavoidable presence of change. Developing resilience is not about trying to control every aspect of life but understanding that change is integral to the human experience. The key lies in recognizing that, although they may not be able to manipulate every circumstance, they possess the power to influence and regulate their responses to change.

The guiding principle in cultivating emotional resilience is acknowledging that change is an inherent and constant force in life. Rather than resisting the natural ebb and flow of circumstances, you can empower yourself by embracing the idea that change is essential to personal growth and development. Life is dynamic and filled with transitions; not everything can be controlled.

In navigating the twists and turns of life, the empowering response is recognizing that, while external events may be beyond control, how one responds to change is within one agency. You develop resilience by consciously choosing how to react to life's uncertainties. It's about fostering a mindset that views change as an opportunity for learning and adaptation rather than a threat.

You must adopt strategies to adapt and thrive in the face of change. This may involve developing flexible problem-solving skills, cultivating a positive mindset, and seeking support from friends, family, or mentors during challenging times. Additionally, engaging in activities that promote self-reflection and emotional expression can enhance one's ability to navigate change with resilience.

Developing a Growth Mindset and Supportive Relationships

Developing a growth mindset is also important for your sense of resilience. This involves transforming setbacks into valuable learning experiences rather than seeing them as insurmountable obstacles.

Encourage a mindset that views challenges not as roadblocks but as stepping stones for personal growth. Embracing this perspective means understanding that every setback presents a unique opportunity to gain new insights, skills, and strengths, contributing significantly to the development of resilience.

The foundation of emotional resilience lies within supportive relationships. You must intentionally surround yourself with friends and family, creating a positive and nurturing environment. These social connections serve as crucial anchors, providing stability during challenging times.

Coping Mechanisms for Various Situations

Life unfolds as an unpredictable journey, presenting many challenges and diverse situations. In the face of this unpredictability, possessing a diverse repertoire of coping mechanisms is akin to having a well-stocked toolkit.

As highlighted by the BetterHelp Editorial Team (2021, para. 1), "Teens experience a higher level of stress than adults do during the school year, and 34% of teens believe their stress will increase over the next year." This underscores the importance of recognizing life's uncertainties and being equipped with effective coping strategies to manage the heightened stress that adolescents often encounter, particularly during the school year.

- **Scenario:** Dealing with academic stress (overwhelming assignments, exams, other academic pressures).
    - **Coping mechanisms**
        - **Time management:** Break down tasks into manageable chunks and prioritize effectively.
        - **Breaks and self-care:** Schedule regular breaks, indulge in enjoyable activities, and prioritize self-care practices.

- **Seek support:** Don't hesitate to contact teachers, classmates, or counselors for academic guidance and support.

- **Scenario:** Navigating relationship challenges when friendships, family dynamics, or romantic relationships pose personal challenges.

    - **Coping mechanisms**

        - **Communication:** Open and honest communication is vital. Express your feelings, thoughts, and concerns calmly and actively listen to others.

        - **Setting boundaries:** Establish clear and healthy boundaries to ensure a balanced and respectful dynamic in your relationships.

        - **Conflict resolution:** Learn practical conflict resolution skills, such as compromise and finding common ground, to address issues constructively.

- **Scenario:** Learning how to manage anxiety and stress from daily life pressures

    - **Coping mechanisms**

        - **Deep breathing** Practice breathing exercises to calm the nervous system and reduce stress.

        - **Positive Thinking:** Engage in positive thinking by consciously filling your mind with good, honorable, upright things to stay present and alleviate anxiety.

- **Physical activity:** Regular exercise releases endorphins, reducing stress and boosting overall mood.

• **Scenario:** Coping with loss or grief when dealing with losing a loved one or a significant life change.

  ○ **Coping mechanisms**

    - **Grieving process:** Allow yourself to grieve, acknowledging and expressing your emotions—seeking support from friends, family, or grief counseling.

    - **Memorializing:** Create memorials to honor and remember the person or situation, fostering a sense of closure.

    - **Journaling:** Express your feelings through writing, providing an outlet for processing emotions during grief.

• **Scenario:** Facing major life transitions, such as moving, changing schools, or starting a new phase in life.

  ○ **Coping mechanisms**

    - **Positive perspective:** Focus on potential personal growth and new opportunities with the transition.

    - **Social connection:** Build a support network in the new environment, connecting with peers, mentors, or community groups.

- **Planning and preparation:** Organize and plan aspects of the transition, which can provide a sense of control and reduce anxiety.

- **Scenario:** Handling peer pressure when you feel pressured to conform to others' expectations.

  o **Coping mechanisms**

    - **Assertiveness:** Practice assertive communication to confidently express your needs, opinions, and boundaries.

    - **Self-reflection:** Understand your values and priorities, enabling you to resist negative influences that may conflict with your principles.

    - **Peer support:** Surround yourself with friends who share positive values and goals, providing a supportive network to lean on.

- **Scenario:** Dealing with uncertainty when facing an uncertain future or unexpected changes.

  o **Coping mechanisms**

    - **Adaptability:** Embrace change as a natural part of life and focus on adapting positively to new circumstances.

    - **Goal setting:** Set short-term goals to maintain a sense of direction, even in uncertain times.

- **Seeking guidance:** Consult with mentors, advisors, or professionals for guidance during periods of uncertainty.

Remember, coping mechanisms are personal, and what works for one person may differ for another. Building a resilient toolkit involves exploration and self-discovery. Feel free to adapt and experiment with these coping strategies based on your unique needs and preferences. By cultivating diverse coping mechanisms, you empower yourself to face life's challenges with resilience, strength, and a positive mindset.

Chapter 4:

Goal Setting and Planning

Imagine this: You're standing on the shore, gazing at the horizon, wondering about the incredible adventures that await. Goals point you toward those adventures. They are the wind in your sails. But what exactly is a goal? And why is it so important to set them?

What Is a Goal?

Think of a goal as more than a finish line—a powerful force driving your journey. It's your guiding light, showing the way to your dreams—a clear target that turns big dreams into a doable roadmap. Goals are like anchors, keeping you grounded, and the North Star guides your ship through the vast sea of possibilities.

Setting goals gives your daily actions a purpose, turning everyday stuff into steps toward something unique. They are your biggest fans, cheering you on when things get tough. They light a fire inside, turning problems into chances and setbacks into epic comebacks. Every goal you hit gives you momentum for the next exciting adventure.

Imagine goals as a lighthouse cutting through the fog, guiding your ship safely to shore. They help you focus, making decisions that match your dreams. Goals clarify the sometimes confusing waters of not knowing what's next.

Goal setting isn't just about reaching a finish line; it's a journey of discovering who you are and growing. Challenges become chances to learn, and setbacks become the winds that push you forward with new strength and toughness.

As the Boys & Girls Clubs of America (2022, para. 2) put it, "Goals help you focus on the journey to whatever you want to achieve, helping them to make plans, use their time and resources wisely, and identify the places where they may need some help."

Setting Clear Goals

Like plotting a course for a grand adventure, establishing clear goals is your roadmap to financial success. In this section, we'll delve into the art of goal-setting, guiding you through defining both short-term objectives and long-term aspirations.

Let's start with the here-and-now—short-term objectives. These are like checkpoints in your financial journey, providing a sense of accomplishment and fueling your motivation. Clearly define short-term financial goals, such as saving for that tech gadget you've been eyeing, funding a memorable trip with friends, or contributing to a passion project that ignites your creativity. Short-term goals are the stepping stones that propel you forward and make the financial journey exciting and rewarding.

Now, let's cast our gaze into the future. Envision your long-term aspirations, those grand dreams that shape the course of your financial odyssey. Whether funding higher education to pursue your passion, venturing into entrepreneurship to bring your ideas to life, or making impactful contributions to causes you deeply care about, long-term goals provide a sense of purpose and direction. They serve as the guiding stars that inspire and drive your financial decisions.

The key to success lies in setting goals that are not only clear but also achievable. Break down your objectives into smaller, manageable steps, creating a roadmap that leads to success. Celebrate each milestone, fueling your motivation to reach the next one. Regularly revisit and adjust your goals as circumstances evolve, ensuring they align with your aspirations.

Setting clear goals is also your secret weapon on the path to financial success. Whether it's short-term objectives that keep you motivated in the present or long-term aspirations that fuel your dreams for the future, goal-setting is the compass that guides your financial journey. So, dream big, set your goals clearly, and watch as each achievement brings you one step closer to the economic future you envision.

The Power of Goal Setting: An Eye-Opening Example

Meet Alex, a teenager with a passion for storytelling. Alex's dream? To write a novel and share it with the world. Without goals, this dream might linger in "someday." But with an objective in mind, like writing one chapter a week, Alex turns that dream into a concrete plan.

Each week, as Alex diligently writes, a magical transformation occurs. The dream takes shape, characters come to life, and a story unfolds like an intricate tapestry. By the end of the year, a novel stands proudly, a testament to the power of setting goals.

This tale of Alex is a testament to the magic that happens when dreams meet goals. So, dear adventurers, get ready to set sail. As we navigate the seas of goal setting, remember that each goal is a star in your constellation, guiding you toward the extraordinary life you envision. The journey begins now!

Understanding SMART Goals for Teens

SMART goals are a framework that encourages creating Specific, Measurable, Achievable, Relevant, and Time-bound objectives. Setting and achieving goals is a fundamental skill that lays the foundation for success in various aspects of life.

SMART goals provide a clear roadmap, helping you define your goals. This clarity is essential when you navigate the most complex academic, social, and personal landscapes you have faced in your life so far.

Measurable goals allow you to track your progress systematically. Seeing tangible results, such as the number of books read or improved grades, provides continuous motivation. It transforms the reading journey into a series of achievable milestones.

The time-bound nature of SMART goals teaches you valuable time management skills. It instills the importance of setting deadlines and prioritizing tasks, essential skills that will serve you well in academics and future careers.

Learning to set and achieve SMART goals prepares you for the challenges you will face as you transition into adulthood. Whether preparing for college, pursuing a career, or navigating personal relationships, the skills developed through SMART goal-setting are invaluable.

- **Specific:**
    - Clearly define the goal. Ask yourself who is involved, what you want to accomplish, where it will happen, when it will be achieved, and why it's essential.

- Instead of a vague goal like "Improve grades," specify it as "Achieve an A grade in math by attending extra tutoring sessions and completing weekly practice problems."

- The specificity of SMART goals aids in academic success. For instance, setting a goal like "Read and analyze one classic novel per month" is more likely to help you excel in literature classes. This level of specificity fosters a deeper engagement with academic material.

- **Measurable:**

  - Establish concrete criteria for measuring progress. This involves quantifying or using observable indicators to track your achievements.

  - Rather than a general goal such as "Read more," make it measurable with "Read two books per month." This way, you can easily track your progress.

- **Achievable:**

  - Given your current resources, skills, and limitations, ensure the goal is realistic and feasible. It should be challenging yet attainable with effort and commitment. The achievability aspect of SMART goals is particularly beneficial for you. Setting realistic challenges ensures that goals are within reach with effort and dedication. This approach fosters a healthy sense of achievement, promoting a positive attitude toward learning and personal growth.

- If you're new to fitness, setting an achievable goal might be "Run a 5k within the next three months" instead of attempting a marathon immediately.

- **Relevant:**

    - Align the goal with your values, interests, and overarching objectives. Ensure that it makes sense in the context of your aspirations.

    - If community service is essential to you, a relevant goal could be "Volunteer at a local shelter twice a month."

- **Time-bound:**

    - Set a specific timeframe for achieving the goal. This creates urgency, turning the goal into a more actionable plan.

    - Make it time-bound instead of a vague timeline with "Achieve conversational proficiency in Spanish within six months" if your goal is language learning.

You can create well-defined, realistic, and motivating objectives by incorporating these SMART criteria into your goal-setting process. This framework provides a structured approach that enhances focus, accountability, and the likelihood of successful goal attainment.

Creating Action Plans

Strategic Thinking

Your goals are not isolated islands but interconnected points on a map. Schedule regular reflections on your long-term vision, ensuring that your short-term objectives align with the overarching direction you want to move in. Strategic thinking keeps you on course.

Breaking Down Goals into Objectives

Think of your goals as towering mountains—formidable yet conquerable when broken down into climbable peaks. Establish a hierarchy by breaking down long-term goals into manageable short-term objectives. These will be the milestones that help you conquer your goals.

The Anatomy of an Action Plan

Your action plan is not a mere roadmap; it's a blueprint for success. Identify tasks, specify the steps required for each objective, and create a detailed task list as a roadmap for action. Prioritize tasks based on urgency, importance, or dependencies. Assign realistic deadlines, allocate resources wisely, and regularly review and adjust your plan as needed.

Cultivating Habits for Success

Identify habits that align with your goals, for consistent habits build momentum. Integrate them into your daily routine, creating a foundation for sustained success. Habits are the quiet allies that transform aspirations into reality.

Balancing Long-Term Vision and Short-Term Objectives

Navigating the goal-setting path is like embarking on a thrilling adventure where your aspirations become the compass guiding your journey. But, just like any journey, it's essential to balance the excitement of the present and the vision of the future.

Picture short-term objectives as the checkpoints in your journey. These small wins keep you motivated, boost your confidence, and offer a taste of achievement along the way. Whether acing a test, mastering a new skill, or completing a project, these short-term victories act as stepping stones toward your larger aspirations.

Long-term goals, on the other hand, guide your overall direction. They provide a sense of purpose and vision, helping you stay focused on what truly matters to you. Think of them as the destination on the horizon, compelling you to push forward, even when the path gets challenging.

Dividing lofty long-term goals into manageable, bite-sized tasks makes them less daunting. Tackling these smaller tasks becomes your detailed roadmap to success, making the grand vision more achievable.

Milestones are not just markers on the journey but celebrations of progress. Acknowledge and celebrate achievements, both big and small. Recognition and reinforcement are the fuel that propels you toward the next milestone. Each celebration is a testament to your commitment, boosting motivation and providing a profound sense of accomplishment.

Life is dynamic, and so are your goals. Be open to reassessing and adjusting your objectives based on evolving circumstances. Flexibility is key to successful goal-setting, allowing you to navigate detours while staying true to your overarching vision.

Set aside dedicated time to reflect on your journey regularly. This practice helps you assess your progress, learn from your experiences, and make informed decisions about adjusting your goals.

The Sweet Spot: Where Short-Term and Long-Term Meet

The real magic unfolds at the intersection of short-term wins and long-term vision. Each small victory becomes a vital building block, constructing the bridge that leads you toward your broader ambitions. Balancing short-term objectives with long-term goals transforms the journey into an exciting and sustainable adventure. It ensures that every step you take brings you closer to the extraordinary future you envision.

So, as you set sail on your goal-setting expedition, remember to cherish the present victories while keeping an eye on the captivating horizon of your long-term dreams. The balance you strike will make your journey more enjoyable and ensure that every step you take brings you closer to the extraordinary future you envision.

Chapter 5:

The Basics of Personal Finance

It's time to unravel the world of credit, loans, and financial planning for the future.

Why Does Personal Finance Matter?

Envision yourself navigating life's choices with personal finance as your guide, ensuring smooth navigation, steering clear of financial challenges, and ultimately reaching the prosperous shores of your dreams. Whether aiming for a first car, saving for college, or envisioning homeownership, understanding the fundamentals of personal finance becomes your passport to financial independence.

Consider personal finance as the guiding chart for your financial journey. It empowers you to make informed decisions, helping you avoid financial pitfalls and stay on course toward your aspirations. Knowledge is power; in finance, it's like possessing your treasure map—an invaluable tool leading you toward the coveted destination of financial freedom.

Imagine personal finance as the solid foundation upon which the structure of your future stands. It's not just about managing money for the present; it's about constructing a groundwork that supports the life you envision living.

Knowledge about budgeting, saving, and wise spending is the key that unlocks the door to financial independence. It grants you the autonomy to make choices aligned with your goals, desires, and values. Circumstances no longer dictate your financial decisions; instead, they become intentional steps toward the life you want to live. Personal finance is not just about having money; it's about having the freedom to choose how you allocate, save, and invest it—a liberating power that shapes your financial destiny.

Financial knowledge is a passport that opens doors to a world of choices. It goes beyond merely accumulating wealth; it allows you to decide how you want to shape your financial landscape. Whether creating an emergency fund to weather unexpected twists, funding your pursuit of higher education, or laying the groundwork for your dream endeavors, personal finance equips you with the tools to navigate life's unpredictable adventures.

Like a practical toolkit, personal finance provides you with the skills to navigate life's twists seamlessly. Whether you face financial emergencies or set the stage for your dream endeavors, a solid understanding of personal finance ensures you are well-prepared for the diverse challenges and opportunities life presents.

Personal finance is not just about managing money; it's about creating a plan that resonates with the melody of your aspirations. So, set a course for prosperity, and let personal finance be your guiding star in the vast sea of financial freedom. The adventure awaits!

As emphasized by the United Way NCA (2023, para. 2), "Equipping young people with the tools to manage their money effectively helps them avoid the cycle of debt and economic insecurity that plagues many Americans well into adulthood, giving them the foundation to build a secure financial future." Furthermore, they highlight that "knowledge of financial concepts like saving, investing, spending, and borrowing is the foundation of financial literacy" (United Way NCA, 2023, para. 5).

The Journey Ahead: Basics of Personal Finance

Embarking on your financial journey is like setting sail on a grand expedition, and the first leg of our adventure involves unraveling the essential pillars of personal finance. These principles act as your compass, guiding you through uncharted territories and enabling you to navigate the complex waters of financial management with confidence and wisdom.

Budgeting, Saving, and Spending Wisely

Budgeting is not a confining restraint. Instead, it gives you the freedom to allocate your resources wisely and purposefully.

Creating a budget is not about confining your dreams; it's about setting sail toward your financial aspirations with purpose and clarity.

In the era of smartphones and endless possibilities, leverage technology to your advantage. Explore a variety of budgeting apps or online spreadsheets that transform the sometimes daunting task of managing your finances into a seamless and even enjoyable experience.

Technology gives you real-time insights into your spending patterns and helps you stay on course with minimal effort.

Picture your spending as a treasure map with various islands representing different categories. Categorization is your map legend, guiding you through the diverse landscape of your financial terrain.

Draw a clear line between necessities (the must-haves) and discretionary expenses (the nice-to-haves). This distinction offers a panoramic view of your financial landscape, allowing you to make informed decisions on where adjustments can be made.

Categorization provides a bird's-eye view of your financial kingdom, empowering you to prioritize and allocate resources wisely.

Establishing realistic spending limits is like plotting your course on budgeting.

When setting limits for discretionary categories, be mindful of your financial goals. Ensure these limits allow for enjoyment while safeguarding your savings' treasure chest.

Realistic limits provide the guardrails for your financial journey, preventing overspending and steering you toward the economic treasures you seek.

Effective Saving

Effective saving is the key to unlocking those vaults if you've ever dreamed of amassing a treasure trove to fund your adventures or aspirations.

Imagine your savings as a fortress, guarding different treasures—emergencies, education, and personal desires. Open separate savings accounts for each goal, creating distinct vaults for your financial aspirations.

- **Emergency fund:** This fund acts as a fortress to keep you safe from unexpected storms. Put aside a portion of your savings to an emergency fund, ensuring you're well-prepared for any financial storm.

- **Education fund:** Whether college or skill-building courses, designate a savings account for your educational pursuits.

- **Personal desires fund:** A treasure chest for your dreams and desires. Allocate funds for personal goals like a dream gadget, a particular trip, or any other cherished wish.

Designating separate accounts provides a clear blueprint for your savings, allowing you to see each fortress's growth and ensuring funds are allocated where needed.

Navigate the seas of saving quickly by automating transfers from your checking to savings accounts. This is like setting your financial ship on auto-pilot—consistent, reliable, and requiring minimal effort.

Schedule regular transfers that go with your budget and income cycle. This ensures a portion of your earnings consistently finds its way into your savings account without you having to give it another thought or wait for you to lift a finger.

Periodically don your financial explorer hat and review your map. Regularly reevaluate your progress, adjusting savings goals based on changing circumstances or new dreams on the horizon.

In the beginning, set a calendar reminder to review your savings strategy every few months. This ensures your financial map remains aligned with your evolving goals and circumstances.

Regular evaluations keep your savings strategy strong, adapting to new opportunities and unexpected challenges or refining your course toward a more prosperous financial future.

Responsible Credit Use

Making informed and responsible decisions about your credit usage is crucial. This section is tailored just for you, providing tips and tricks on confidently navigating the world of credit.

Before diving into the credit card game, take the time to do your homework. Thoroughly research different credit cards, comparing interest rates, fees, and benefits. Look for cards with low interest rates and reasonable prices to ensure you're setting yourself up for financial success from the start.

Once you've selected the right credit card, resist the urge to go shopping. Instead, start small by using your credit card for routine purchases like groceries or school supplies. By keeping your purchases manageable, you'll be better equipped to pay off the balance in full each month. This helps you avoid accumulating debt and establishes a positive credit history, which is critical for future financial endeavors.

Building responsible credit habits starts with commitment. Make it a personal rule to pay off your credit card balance in full every month. This prevents interest charges from piling up and demonstrates to lenders that you are a reliable borrower. Consistency is vital, so stay disciplined in your approach to credit use.

As you start your credit journey, make it a habit to monitor your credit score regularly. Celebrate positive changes and improvements in your score, and promptly address any discrepancies or issues. Regular credit monitoring not only keeps you informed about your financial standing but also empowers you to take control of your credit health.

Responsible credit use is a skill that will serve you well throughout your life. By conducting thorough research, making minor and routine purchases, committing to responsible habits, and regularly monitoring your credit, you'll be well on your way to building a solid and positive credit history. Take charge of your financial future, and remember, smart decisions today lead to a brighter tomorrow. Happy credit navigating!

Financial Goal Setting: Navigating Your Wealth Map

The first step toward financial triumph involves gaining crystal-clear clarity on your goals. Whether your ambitions include saving for the latest gadget, planning for your college education, or envisioning your first car, articulating your goals distinctly lays out the roadmap for your financial expedition. Jot them down and place them where you can regularly revisit them, constantly reminding you of your financial destination.

While monumental financial goals may seem daunting, fear not! The key lies in dissecting them into smaller, bite-sized fragments. Instead of fixating on the entire mountain, focus on the initial climbing steps. For example, if your objective is to save for college, break it down into manageable steps such as researching scholarship opportunities, setting a monthly savings target, and exploring part-time job options. This approach transforms your goals into more digestible tasks, making them less overwhelming and more achievable.

Life is a dynamic journey, and so are your financial circumstances. Regularly reviewing and adjusting your financial goals must align with your evolving aspirations. Dedicate a few months to assess your progress, revel in your achievements, and reassess your objectives. Are there new opportunities or challenges on the horizon? Tailor your goals accordingly to stay on course and sustain motivation.

Informed Investing

The world of investing is both thrilling and full of opportunities. Whether you're dreaming of financial independence, planning for your education, or simply looking to grow your wealth, informed investing is the key to unlocking your economic potential.

To become a savvy investor, immerse yourself in investment options. Explore the dynamics of stocks, bonds, and mutual funds. Understand how the market operates, what factors influence the values of different investments, and the potential risks associated with each option. Utilize reputable financial resources, online platforms, and educational materials to build a solid foundation of knowledge. The more you understand, the better equipped you'll be to make informed decisions.

While self-education is crucial, there's immense value in seeking the expertise of a financial advisor. A professional can offer personalized advice tailored to your unique financial situation. Whether you're a newcomer to investing or looking to refine your strategy, a financial advisor can provide insights, answer questions, and align your investment choices with your specific goals. Think of them as your financial mentor, helping you navigate the complexities of the market.

Start small by investing amounts you're comfortable with, allowing you to gain hands-on experience without exposing yourself to undue risk. As you become more confident and knowledgeable, gradually diversify your portfolio. Diversification helps spread risk across different assets, safeguarding your investments from the fluctuations of any single market. Consider combining stocks, bonds, and other investment vehicles to create a well-rounded and resilient portfolio.

The world of investing is dynamic and ever-changing. Stay engaged with ongoing education, keeping up-to-date with market trends, economic developments, and changes in investment landscapes. Regularly monitor your investments and assess their performance against your financial goals. This proactive approach enables you to adjust your portfolio as needed, ensuring it remains aligned with your evolving aspirations.

Informed investing is a journey of growth, empowerment, and financial well-being. By researching investment options, seeking professional advice, starting small while diversifying gradually, and embracing continuous learning and monitoring, you're setting the stage for a prosperous financial future. Embrace the excitement of the investment world, stay informed, and watch your wealth flourish over time.

Understanding Credit and Loans

As you work toward your financial independence, understanding the dynamic duo of credit and loans will be instrumental in shaping your financial destiny—picture credit and loans as your allies, ready to accompany you through life's adventures.

Consider credit as your loyal financial sidekick, always by your side to help you achieve your dreams. Like any companion, it demands your attention and understanding. The better you understand the nuances of credit, the more effectively you can leverage it to your advantage. Whether you're dreaming of starting a small business, pursuing higher education, or making a significant purchase, credit can be the catalyst that transforms your aspirations into tangible achievements.

Building Credit Responsibly

There is an art to building credit responsibly—a skill that will set the stage for a bright financial future. Think of this process as crafting your financial superhero cape, symbolizing your ability to navigate the economic landscape confidently.

If the prospect of a credit card intrigues you, approach it strategically. Use your credit card for small, routine purchases—consider it a financial training ground where you can hone your money management skills. The golden rule here is to pay off the balance in full each month. This shields you from accumulating interest charges and creates a positive credit history.

Why is a positive credit history so important to you? It's essentially a collection of badges showcasing your financial responsibility. Your strategic use of a credit card contributes to this positive history, signaling to lenders that you are a reliable borrower. This upbeat track record becomes a valuable asset when you're ready to take on major life milestones, such as securing a loan for a car, financing your education, or even purchasing your dream home.

Understanding credit and loans is a pivotal chapter in your financial adventure. By strategically using credit cards for small purchases and consistently paying them off, you're not just building a positive credit history—you're sculpting the foundation for a robust and resilient financial future. So, fasten your seatbelt, embrace the twists and turns of your financial journey, and let credit be your trusty companion as you unlock a world of possibilities.

Financial Planning for the Future

As you stand at the threshold of your future, envision it as an expansive canvas awaiting the vibrant strokes of your financial planning. This leg of our journey transcends the immediacy of day-to-day expenses, delving into legacy crafting and aspirations that resonate far beyond the present moment.

Investing Wisely

Think of investing as planting seeds for your financial garden, and in this section, we'll explore two critical principles: diversification and time horizon.

Imagine you have a garden, and each plant represents a different investment. If a sudden frost hits and damages one type of plant, the others may still thrive. This concept of spreading risk is diversification. In the investment world, it means exploring various asset classes to ensure your portfolio remains resilient to market fluctuations.

Suppose you have $1,000 to invest. Consider diversifying across different assets instead of putting it all into one stock. Allocate a portion to stocks, bonds, and perhaps a mutual fund. If one investment experiences a downturn, the others may help offset the losses, providing a more balanced and stable portfolio.

Your time horizon is like the seasons in your financial garden. Some plants bloom quickly, while others take time to grow and flourish. Similarly, your investments should align with both short-term and long-term financial goals.

Let's say you'll save for a new laptop next year. For this short-term goal, consider low-risk investments like a certificate of deposit (CD) or a short-term bond. Conversely, if you dream of starting your own business in ten years, you can afford to take on more risk with long-term investments like stocks. The longer time horizon allows your money to ride out market fluctuations and yield higher returns.

It's important to always invest with a sense of purpose. Your financial goals should guide your investment decisions. Regularly review and adjust your portfolio to align with your evolving plans.

As you progress through high school and college, your goals may shift. Initially, you might save for a car (short-term goal), but later, your focus could be funding your college education or starting a small business (long-term goal). Adjust your investment strategy accordingly, moving from short-term, low-risk investments to a mix that supports your evolving aspirations.

Like tending to a garden, nurturing your investments with purpose and strategy is critical. By diversifying your portfolio and aligning investments with your time horizon, you're setting the stage for a financially fruitful future. So, plant your investment seeds wisely, adapt to the changing seasons of life, and watch your financial garden thrive.

Seeing Planning in Action

Meet Emily, a passionate young artist with dreams of making a positive impact through her creativity. Initially, financial planning might seem disconnected from her artistic pursuits, but its significance becomes clear as she explores the possibilities.

Emily's short-term goal is to attend an art workshop that aligns with her unique style. By allocating a portion of her earnings from a part-time job, she ensures that her financial decisions are about managing expenses and investing in her passions.

As Emily learns about investment options, she discovers opportunities to invest in art funds that support emerging artists. Her financial choices grow her wealth and contribute to the community she aims to be a part of.

Considering the long-term impact of her choices, Emily begins to explore estate planning options. She envisions establishing an art scholarship or foundation that sustains and supports budding artists, ensuring her artistic legacy endures.

In Emily's story, financial planning bridges immediate aspirations and a future adorned with possibilities. Each financial decision represents a deliberate and purposeful action steering her toward economic empowerment and resilience.

Why It Matters

Financial planning equips teens like Emily with the tools to navigate life's unexpected twists. Whether it's seizing incredible opportunities or weathering economic storms, having a well-thought-out plan provides a sense of stability and control.

Planning for the future financially empowers teens to pursue their dreams with vigor. Emily's passion for art is not merely a hobby; it becomes a guiding force shaping her career choices, lifestyle, and contributions to the artistic community.

Crafting a legacy is not confined to financial inheritances alone. It's about leaving an indelible mark on the world, contributing to causes that matter, and ensuring that your values echo through generations.

Chapter 6:

Problem Solving and Critical Thinking

Harness the power of problem-solving and critical thinking to navigate challenges skillfully, analyze situations with clarity, and make informed decisions that pave the way for your success—picture life as a puzzle, with each challenge serving as a piece waiting to be placed. Problem-solving is not merely about finding solutions; it is vital to unlocking doors to growth, resilience, and success.

After all, "Good decision-making skills can set you up for success later in life. Additionally, good decision-making skills help you manage your stress levels better" (Morin, 2019, para. 3).

Empowering Decision-Making

Being a teenager means facing many choices, from shaping your academic journey to navigating the intricacies of relationships. Every decision becomes an opportunity for your personal growth. Empowering decision-making enables exploration of interests, discovery of strengths, and understanding of values, contributing to a robust foundation for your future self.

Take, for example, when you need to speak publicly for a school project. Despite being outside your comfort zone, embracing the challenge becomes a chance for personal growth and raising confidence in your abilities.

Decisions made during your teen years carry significant weight for your future. Take, for example, the decision to choose a specific elective course. Though seemingly minor, it sets the stage for potential future interests, career paths, and educational pursuits.

The ability to make and stand by decisions builds confidence. When you make decisions, you learn to trust your judgment, especially when facing challenges. Confidence is more than just a good trait; it's necessary for a healthy, well-adjusted adult.

As a teen, you must manage peer pressure and societal expectations. Empowering decision-making becomes your shield against external forces, allowing choices that resonate with your authentic self and fostering a sense of independence and individuality.

It's not hard to visualize a scenario where friends engage in activities that make you uncomfortable. You can combat engaging in those situations by making decisions that honor how you feel.

In the context of brain development, the American Academy of Child and Adolescent Psychiatry (2017) notes that adolescents differ from adults in behavior, problem-solving, and decision-making. Biological studies reveal ongoing brain maturation throughout childhood, adolescence, and early adulthood. Specific brain regions like the amygdala, responsible for immediate reactions, develop early, while the frontal cortex, governing reasoning, develops later and continues changing into adulthood. Other changes during adolescence, such as increased brain connections and myelin development, are crucial for coordinated thought and behavior. Research indicates that adolescents' brains work differently than adults during decision-making, with actions being more guided by the emotional and reactive amygdala than the thoughtful frontal cortex. Substance exposure during the teen years can alter or delay these developmental processes.

How to Make Empowered Decisions

Begin by understanding yourself—your values, interests, and aspirations. Reflect on past decisions and their outcomes. What did you learn from them? This self-awareness forms the basis for making decisions that align with your authentic self.

Journal about your interests, strengths, and what brings you joy. This provides you with a clearer understanding of your preferences, aiding you in making decisions that align with your authentic self.

Gather Information

Empowering decision-making is informed decision-making. Decision-making is a deliberate and conscious effort to sift through the possibilities of every choice and consider each choice's consequences.

The first step involves carefully examining all of your available options. It requires a keen awareness of all the paths before you. Allowing yourself to contemplate the details of each choice lets you truly understand where each path will ultimately bring you.

No matter how seemingly insignificant, every decision has a ripple effect that resonates through various aspects of your life. Confident choices will impact your relationships, professional endeavors, and overall well-being. There is no denying that you have to learn how to weigh each choice's potential pitfalls and rewards.

Knowledge is crucial for informed decision-making. Invest time in gathering relevant information about the available choices. This may involve research, seeking expert advice, or drawing on personal experiences. A comprehensive understanding of options ensures that decisions are grounded in reality rather than speculation.

Identify and prioritize your core values and take time for reflection. Align decisions with principles that matter most to you, ensuring choices resonate with your authentic self and contribute positively to overall well-being. Reflect on feelings, motivations, and potential biases that may influence your decision. Values act as a guiding force, directing decisions in line with fundamental beliefs.

Explore alternative courses of action. Assessing a range of options allows you to choose the one that aligns best with your goals and values. This step prevents tunnel vision and encourages creative thinking, fostering a more thorough and nuanced decision-making process.

Armed with a thorough understanding of goals, relevant information, and considerations of consequences, make the decision. Acknowledge that informed decisions aren't always about certainty but about making choices based on the best available information and thoughtful consideration.

Once the decision is made, implement it with commitment. Be prepared to adapt as circumstances evolve and remain open to learning from outcomes. The ability to adjust the course based on feedback and experiences is vital to the decision-making journey.

Research different career paths, talk to professionals in those fields, and explore the educational requirements. This information empowers you to make informed decisions about your academic and career choices.

Seek Guidance

Don't hesitate to seek guidance from trusted mentors, parents, or friends. Discussing your thoughts with others can provide valuable insights and different perspectives. It's not about relinquishing control but enriching your decision-making process with diverse viewpoints.

Before making a significant decision, seek advice from a teacher, mentor, or family member. Their experiences and perspectives can offer valuable insights to a more well-rounded decision-making process.

Consider Long-Term Goals

Making informed decisions extends beyond the immediate circumstances. When you make a more informed decision, you consider the choice against your long-term vision and aspirations. What impact will this decision have on your future ambitions? Empowering decision-making involves looking beyond immediate gratification and understanding the broader implications of your choices. Aligning your options with your long-term goals ensures that today's decisions contribute meaningfully to the broader trajectory of your life, letting you navigate it with a sense of purpose and foresight.

If you aspire to pursue a career in environmental science, consider how your lifestyle choices, such as reducing waste or choosing sustainable products, align with that long-term goal.

Embrace Mistakes as Learning Opportunities

Empowering decision-making doesn't mean perfection. Mistakes are inevitable and, more importantly, invaluable learning opportunities. Embrace them, analyze what went wrong, and use that knowledge to refine your decision-making skills for the future.

If a decision leads to unexpected challenges, view it as a learning opportunity. Analyze what factors contributed to the outcome and use that knowledge to approach similar decisions with greater insight.

Navigating the Maze of Challenges

Challenges may seem like insurmountable roadblocks, casting shadows on your journey. However, challenges are not dead ends but opportunities in disguise.

Adolescence is a period of rapid growth and change, both physically and emotionally. Learning to navigate challenges builds resilience—the ability to bounce back from setbacks. Resilience is a cornerstone for mental well-being, helping you face adversities with strength and adaptability.

Challenges often involve interpersonal conflicts, especially among friends. Learning to navigate these conflicts builds essential skills in conflict resolution. This strengthens relationships and equips you to manage disputes in your life.

Learning to navigate challenges instills adaptability and flexibility. Knowing how to adapt will make you better equipped to face future uncertainties. Challenges are, fundamentally, problems waiting to be solved. Navigating challenges builds problem-solving competence. Those with a problem-solving mindset are better equipped to tackle academic, personal, and professional hurdles.

How to Successfully Navigate Challenges in a Healthy Way

Cultivate a positive mindset by viewing challenges as opportunities for growth. Embrace the idea that overcoming challenges builds resilience and character, transforming them from obstacles into stepping stones.

Don't face challenges alone. Seek support from friends, family, or mentors. Sharing your thoughts and concerns provides emotional help and brings different perspectives.

Break down challenges into smaller, manageable steps. Tackling one aspect at a time makes the overall challenge less overwhelming and helps maintain focus.

View setbacks as learning experiences. Analyze what went wrong, extract valuable lessons, and apply them to future challenges. Every setback is an opportunity for personal and intellectual growth.

Prioritize self-care during challenging times. Ensure you take care of your physical and mental well-being through activities you enjoy, whether reading, exercising, or spending time with loved ones.

Identify and develop healthy coping mechanisms. This could include journaling, art, or engaging in joyous hobbies. Healthy coping mechanisms contribute to emotional well-being during challenging times.

Adopt a growth mindset by believing in your ability to learn and adapt. Understand that challenges are part of the learning process and an opportunity to enhance your skills and capabilities.

Learning to navigate challenges is a fundamental aspect of your development. It goes beyond mere problem-solving; it shapes character, builds resilience, and equips you with the skills needed to thrive in an ever-changing world. Challenges are not roadblocks but invitations to grow, adapt, and emerge stronger on the other side.

Fueling Innovation and Creativity

Problems are not just a puzzle to solve; they're a chance for something to be explored.

Think of creative problem-solving as your superpower for innovation. It's not about sticking to the usual—it's about breaking free, thinking outside the box, and coming up with ideas as unique as you are. Brace yourself for those moments that make you go, "Wow, I never thought of that!"

Imagine you've got a history project. Instead of the same old routine, gather your friends for a brainstorming session. Let your ideas fly—maybe turn your presentation into a mini-movie, complete with music, visuals, and a touch of interactive magic.

Ever felt like a problem is just waiting for your personal touch? Creative problem-solving is your chance to infuse your projects with your personality, interests, and a sprinkle of your unique flair. It's your time to shine!

Break free from the norm by combining things in unexpected ways. Imagine creating your recipe for success in a way that makes your solutions stand out. Creative problem-solving lets you blend knowledge from diverse areas, creating effective and cool solutions.

We're all stars in our show, and creative problem-solving lets you shine even brighter. It's not about fitting in—it's about celebrating what makes you uniquely awesome. Grab your creative paintbrush, dive into the adventure, and turn every challenge into a masterpiece that is uniquely yours. The world's your canvas—what will you paint today?

How to Add Some Creative Spark

- **Think outside the box:** Break free from the usual. Let your mind wander without limits. Who says problems need standard solutions? The more outside the box, the better!

- **Mix things up:** Combine ideas in unexpected ways. It's like creating a fusion dish but for solutions. The weirder, the better—embrace the unexpected!

- **Mind maps are your friend:** Visualize your thoughts with mind maps. It's like creating a path to find those golden ideas. Let your creativity flow freely on paper.

- **Team up for brainstorming sessions:** Get your buddies involved. More brains mean more excellent ideas. Collaborative problem-solving is like having your brainstorming party—an adventure with friends!

- **Try and fail (it's cool!):** Experiment with different approaches. It's not about getting it right first but having fun. Failure is just a stepping stone to excellent solutions.

Building Resilience: Turning Setbacks Into Stepping Stones

Life is filled with exhilarating highs and challenging lows. Due to this whirlwind, problems will undoubtedly arise. So naturally, issues that lead to setbacks will occur. The only way to offset them healthily is to have problem-solving skills and resilience. Resilience is like a soothing balm that heals the wounds of setbacks and turns failures into valuable lessons. With your wound healed, you then have the power to push through with a sense of newfound strength and determination.

Resilience isn't just about bouncing back—it's about transforming adversity into a catalyst for growth. When life throws curveballs your way, resilience becomes the alchemy that turns challenges into opportunities for self-discovery and personal development.

Setbacks are like sudden storms that disrupt the calm of everyday life. In such moments, resilience is your inner fortitude, helps you stand tall amid the chaos, and prepares you for the journey ahead.

Say you've invested your heart and soul into a personal project, only to encounter an unexpected setback. This is where problem-solving steps in, not just as a troubleshooter but as a powerful instrument for building resilience.

The initial step in overcoming failure is analyzing what went wrong. Problem-solving demands a close examination of the situation, identifying the contributing factors to the setback, and gaining a profound understanding of the nuances of the experience.

Resilience is intrinsically tied to the ability to extract lessons from setbacks. Problem-solving goes beyond a quick fix—it involves mining valuable insights from failure and success alike. What worked? What didn't?

How to Build Resilience

Embrace a growth mindset that perceives challenges as opportunities for growth. Resilience thrives when setbacks are seen as stepping stones toward becoming a better you.

Identify and nurture healthy coping mechanisms. Whether seeking solace in conversation, pouring your thoughts into a journal, or engaging in activities that bring joy, effective coping strategies enhance your ability to bounce back from setbacks.

Surround yourself with a supportive network of friends, family, and mentors. Resilience is often bolstered by the encouragement and understanding of those who genuinely care about your well-being.

While aiming high is commendable, setting realistic goals helps manage expectations. Resilience flourishes when goals are challenging yet achievable, allowing for a sense of accomplishment even in the face of setbacks.

Acknowledge and celebrate your progress, no matter how small. Resilience is built incrementally, and recognizing your achievements boosts confidence.

Life is an unpredictable journey, and setbacks are an inevitable part of the ride. However, with resilience as your guide and problem-solving as your trusted companion, setbacks cease to be roadblocks and instead become stepping stones toward personal growth and success. As you confront the unknown, remember that resilience is not just a quality; it's a skill that can be nurtured and strengthened with each challenge you conquer. So, embrace the bumps, learn from the curves, and let resilience be the force that keeps your journey vibrant and full of possibilities. After all, it's not about avoiding the storms but learning to dance in the rain.

The Journey Ahead: Problem Solving and Critical Thinking

Life is filled with various situations. Navigating all these situations requires cultivating a discerning eye, appreciating the nuances, and unraveling patterns that shape your experiences.

Consider, for instance, witnessing a disagreement between friends. In a situation like this, it pays to have problem-solving skills. Those skills transcend mere observation; they involve plunging into the hearts of the matter. When you understand each of your friends' perspectives, you can propose resolutions that address the core issues. It's not merely about resolving a dispute; it's about fostering understanding and harmony.

Creativity extends far beyond the confines of traditional art forms. The dynamic force ignites ingenious solutions. Creativity involves thinking beyond established boundaries, embracing diverse perspectives, and transforming constraints into opportunities. Enabling your inner innovator allows you to discover the magic that unfolds when creativity intertwines with problem-solving.

Creative problem-solving starts with divergent thinking. It's the ability to generate many ideas and explore various perspectives to find innovative solutions. For example, when faced with a challenging school project, brainstorm different approaches and consider unconventional angles to elevate your work.

Creativity is like a playlist made entirely of music from vastly different genres. Imagine you and your friends are planning a party, and everyone has their favorite genre. Creativity is when you mix up all those diverse music styles to create a playlist that everyone can enjoy.

You're organizing a party, and the goal is to have the best music ever. Everyone in your friend group has their own music taste—some are into hip-hop, others love pop, and some are about rock. Instead of sticking to one genre, you all gather and start brainstorming. You blend your music preferences. The result? It's a good playlist with a mix of tracks that wouldn't have happened if you didn't bring all your musical vibes together.

Creativity isn't just about what one person can do alone. It's about bringing all these different tastes and beats into one awesome playlist. It's like making the ultimate music fusion—each genre adds its vibe, and together, it's a party anthem!

Creativity flourishes in ambiguity. It's the willingness to embrace uncertainty and see challenges as opportunities for exploration. In personal growth, navigating life transitions or making significant decisions often involves ambiguity. Embrace the unknown, allowing creative solutions to emerge as you adapt and learn.

Creative problem-solving is all about combining your ideas with others to make something extraordinary happen. Imagine you and your friends teaming up for a community project, like sprucing up a local hangout spot. Working with people who bring different skills and perspectives, such as local artists, tech whizzes, and community members, can lead to cool ideas that cater to everyone's needs. It's like turning a dull space into a vibrant one by blending everyone's creativity!

Creative problem-solving is like fine-tuning your game strategy. Imagine you and your friends are launching a startup, like a new app. It's not a one-shot deal; it's a constant process of tweaking and improving. Like in gaming, where you adjust your tactics based on how the game unfolds, in entrepreneurship, you're constantly refining the business plan, upgrading features, and improving the user experience. It's like leveling up your startup by continuously fine-tuning and adapting—like in your favorite video game!

Instead of sticking to a rigid schedule, get creative! Design a personalized schedule that syncs with your natural energy levels. It's like optimizing your gaming setup for the ultimate experience—you tailor it to suit your style, ensuring you use your energy wisely and level up your success in reaching your goals.

Chapter 7:

Making Friends and Building Relationships

Building connections is an intricate dance, each step contributing to the beautiful choreography of our lives. It's a journey where the spotlight is on you, and the relationships you cultivate become the meaningful notes in the symphony of your life.

Positive friendships are not just about companionship; they provide support and a sense of belonging and can reinforce healthy behaviors. These friendships also contribute to developing positive social skills like cooperation, communication, conflict resolution, and resisting negative peer pressure. Moreover, evidence suggests that positive adolescent friendships lay the groundwork for successful adult relationships, including romantic ones.

According to the Office of Population Affairs (2022), adolescence is a whirlwind of rapid change—physically, emotionally, and socially. Friendships during this period play a vital role as adolescents develop their identity and grapple with self-esteem. In the early stages, the desire to fit in with peers may drive friendships, with youths adapting their interests to match those of their friends. However, youths form more diverse friend groups as adolescence progresses and express their independent preferences within their social circles.

Roehlkepartain et al. (2017) emphasize that young people who experience strong developmental relationships are likelier to report a wide range of social-emotional strengths, contributing to their overall well-being and thriving. These relationships act as a resilience booster, making young individuals more capable of facing stress and trauma. The importance of a strong web of relationships becomes evident as young people fare better when connected to various individuals.

Friends—We Need to Find Them

Finding friends as a teen can be an exciting yet sometimes challenging endeavor. The environments in which you can forge connections are diverse, and the importance of having friends you can trust and feel safe with cannot be overstated.

High school is a melting pot of diverse personalities, creating a fertile ground for cultivating friendships. Shared classes, group projects, and the camaraderie developed during school events often lay the foundation for enduring connections.

Joining clubs or participating in extracurricular activities allows you to engage with like-minded individuals who share similar passions. These shared interests facilitate organic friendships, whether it's a sports team, drama club, or science enthusiasts.

Local events and community gatherings provide an opportunity to connect beyond the school setting. Fairs, festivals, and community service initiatives unite individuals from various backgrounds, fostering friendships with people who might not be part of the daily school routine.

Online platforms offer a virtual space for you to connect. While approaching online friendships cautiously is essential, forums, social media groups, or interest-based websites can help you find others who share niche hobbies or perspectives.

Engaging in volunteer activities not only serves the community but also introduces you to individuals passionate about making a positive impact. Shared values in a volunteer setting can lead to meaningful connections.

Why Trustworthy Friends Matter

Knowing that there's someone to share joys and sorrows with contributes significantly to emotional well-being. Feeling safe and secure within friendships creates an environment where you can authenticate yourself. Trustworthy friends establish a foundation of loyalty and confidentiality, reducing fears of judgment or betrayal.

Friends who align with one's values and interests contribute to a profound sense of belonging. Shared experiences and common ground foster deeper connections, promoting understanding and a genuine appreciation for each other's uniqueness.

Adolescence is marked by significant personal growth and change. Trustworthy friends act as companions on this journey, offering valuable advice, empathy, and shared experiences that help navigate the complexities of this transformative phase.

Friendships are a crucial arena for the development of social skills. Interacting with friends helps you refine communication, empathy, and conflict-resolution skills, providing a valuable foundation for navigating relationships in various aspects of life.

The quest for friends is an integral and dynamic part of your teenage experience. The environments where connections are forged are diverse, and the importance of cultivating friendships with individuals who can be trusted and provide a sense of safety cannot be overstated.

Initiating Conversations

Always remember that initiating conversations marks the initial and exciting step in making new friends. As you approach others with open body language, start with friendly greetings, find common ground, and pose open-ended questions, you're not merely engaging in casual talk but laying the essential groundwork for potential friendships. This process is more than just a social skill; it's the cornerstone of building connections that can evolve into lasting bonds. So, embrace the art of conversation, and let the journey of meaningful friendships unfold.

It's the first step in connecting with someone new, opening the door to potential friendships and shared experiences.

Initiating conversations with others is crucial, especially during your teenage years, when forming connections and friendships contribute to your personal growth and well-being.

Here are just some of the reasons why it's so important:

- **Building connections:** Initiating conversations is the first step in building connections. It's like laying the foundation for meaningful relationships, offering support, companionship, and shared experiences. Having a network of friends can make the teenage journey more enjoyable and less isolating.

- **Developing social skills:** Starting conversations is valuable beyond your teenage years. It's like honing a skill set that will benefit various aspects of life, from school and college to the workplace. Effective communication is a critical component of success in any social setting.

- **Boosting confidence:** Taking the initiative to start a conversation boosts self-confidence. It's like conquering the fear of reaching out to others and realizing that your voice and opinions matter. This newfound confidence can positively impact other areas of life, including academic performance and extracurricular activities.

- **Expanding perspectives**: Conversing with diverse people exposes you to different perspectives and ideas. It's like opening a window to varied experiences and opinions. This exposure broadens your understanding of the world and helps you become more open-minded and empathetic.

How to Begin

Approach With Open Body Language

Open body language refers to nonverbal cues and gestures that convey a sense of approachability, friendliness, and receptiveness in social interactions. It involves using one's body to communicate a positive and welcoming demeanor, making others feel comfortable and encouraged to engage in conversation.

Imagine being at a school event or gathering, eager to connect with someone new. As you scan the crowd, you spot an individual who piques your interest. Before exchanging words, your body language becomes the silent narrator of your approach. It's like the overture to a conversation, setting the tone for potential connections.

Surrounded by peers at a lively school party, how you carry yourself becomes crucial in the unspoken language of connection. Approach the crowd with openness and friendliness—a nonverbal introduction to who you are. Maintain eye contact, a beacon of genuine interest; let your warm smile radiate friendliness, and consciously avoid crossing your arms to broadcast an approachable demeanor. This initial visual communication becomes the prelude to a positive and welcoming interaction.

In both scenarios, the art of approaching with open body language becomes a universal theme. The nonverbal cues you emit become the first chapter of a potential connection, whether at a school event or a bustling party. It's not just about what you say, it's about the unspoken dialogue that conveys your approachability and genuine interest in connecting with others.

Start With a Friendly Greeting

Now, let's unravel the power of a simple "hello"—a surprisingly simple but potent icebreaker. This friendly greeting is more than a formality; it's a genuine invitation to connect, creating a warm conversation handshake. Whether you find yourself in a classroom, at a lively party, or casually passing by someone in the hallway, the impact of this simple gesture should not be underestimated.

Tailoring your greeting to the situation allows warmth to shine through, turning a conventional exchange into a meaningful connection. It's like setting the stage for a positive tone in the conversation, signaling your openness to engage with others. A well-crafted and genuine welcome can make all the difference, transforming a brief interaction into the beginning of a potentially enriching connection. So, the next time you say "hello," recognize it as more than words; it's a powerful initiation.

Find Common Ground

Building connections is all about finding common ground with others. Consider common ground the fertile soil from which connections can flourish. It's like unearthing shared interests that are the foundation for the bonds you create.

Whether at an event, in a class, or meeting someone new, actively seek out these connection points. It could be a shared hobby, a mutual acquaintance, or even a common experience. Finding that common ground transforms the task of initiating a conversation into a smoother, more enjoyable experience.

Consider common ground the glue that binds your initial interaction, making the conversation relatable and enjoyable. It's the shared passion for a favorite band, the joy derived from a similar hobby, or the realization of having a mutual friend. These shared interests become the bridges that span the initial gap, creating pathways to deeper, more meaningful connections.

Ask Open-Ended Questions

Instead of settling for mundane yes or no queries, let's embrace the creativity of questions that invite others to share the depth of their thoughts and experiences. Rather than a routine "How was your weekend?" why not ask, "What was the highlight of your weekend?" This question demonstrates genuine interest and encourages the other person to go into their experiences and share more freely.

Here are a few examples of better questions to ask:

- What's a movie or TV show that you've recently enjoyed and why?

- What's a hobby or activity that truly lights you up, and why does it resonate with you?

- If you could travel anywhere in the world right now, where would it be, and what would you do there?

- What's a dream or goal you have for your future, and what steps are you taking to work toward it?

- Can you share a book that left a lasting impression on you, and what about it resonated with you?

Incorporating these open-ended questions into your conversations transforms the dialogue from routine exchanges into an engaging exploration of thoughts, feelings, and shared experiences. The beauty lies not only in the questions themselves but in the genuine curiosity you bring, fostering connections beyond the surface.

A Story

Meet Jamie, a high school student who initially struggled with reaching out to new people. One day, Jamie was grouped with a student named Taylor during a collaborative school project. Although the prospect of initiating a conversation was daunting, Jamie decided to take a chance and break the ice by asking about Taylor's interests.

Approaching Taylor with open body language, Jamie maintained eye contact, offered a warm smile, and, with a deep breath, ventured into a friendly greeting. "Hey, Taylor! What are your thoughts on this project? Any cool ideas?" The response was beyond expectations—Taylor lit up, sharing thoughts on the project and personal interests that resonated with Jamie.

This simple act of initiating a conversation became the catalyst for a blossoming friendship. Jamie and Taylor discovered common ground in shared hobbies and interests beyond the school project. The two began studying together, and then they started hanging out outside of school--exploring new interests together.

What started as a tentative outreach became a source of positive connections and personal growth for Jamie. The experience of initiating conversations with Taylor led to a newfound friendship and significantly boosted Jamie's confidence and social skills. The fear of reaching out had transformed into a gateway to enriching experiences and lasting connections.

Jamie's story underscores the importance of initiating conversations, demonstrating that taking a chance can open doors to friendships and personal development. It reminds you that stepping out of your comfort zone and starting conversations can lead to meaningful connections and a richer high school experience.

Forming Meaningful Connections

Authenticity is magnetic. Be true to yourself in conversations. Share your thoughts, experiences, and emotions sincerely. Authenticity builds trust and allows others to connect with the real you. Embrace your uniqueness, and let others see the genuine person beneath the surface.

Opening up about your own experiences creates a sense of vulnerability and relatability. It allows others to see your human side and may encourage them to share their stories. Shared experiences form a strong bond, creating a foundation for a deeper connection.

Actively seek opportunities to support others. Whether it's offering assistance, encouragement, or simply being there to listen, offering help builds a sense of camaraderie. Acts of kindness contribute to the development of a supportive and meaningful relationship.

After the initial interaction, make an effort to follow up. Whether it's a quick message, a phone call, or suggesting another meet-up, staying connected reinforces the relationship. Consistency in communication shows that you value the connection and are interested in its growth.

Focus on building a few deep and meaningful connections rather than an extensive network of superficial ones. Quality connections provide a sense of support, understanding, and shared experiences. Investing time and energy into a few significant relationships often yields more profound and lasting connections.

Remember, the journey of forming meaningful connections is a two-way street. Be patient, be genuine, and enjoy the process of building relationships that add depth and richness to your life.

Chapter 8:

Health and Well-being

Your health is the masterpiece that colors every experience, every achievement, and every moment.

The Foundation of Physical Health

Think of your body as a powerhouse of muscles, bones, and energy, all set to rock and roll. Regular exercise isn't just a task; it's your secret weapon to unlock all the awesome potential your body holds. It's not just about being fit; it's about boosting your energy, building resilience, and showing off your strength. And guess what? It's not just a physical thing—it's like a daily boost that makes you feel better in your mind and emotions too.

Regular aerobic exercises, such as brisk walking, jogging, or cycling, compose a love letter to your heart. These activities improve cardiovascular efficiency, promoting circulation and oxygenating every cell. The result? Enhanced endurance, a reduced risk of heart disease, and an overall boost to cardiovascular health.

Similar to a sculptor molding clay into a masterpiece, consistent strength training sculpts and tones your muscles. Resistance exercises, whether utilizing weights or your body weight, contribute to improved muscle tone and strength, fostering better posture and joint health. This increased resilience to physical challenges aligns with your daily activities.

Now, meet endorphins—your body's natural mood lifters. Engaging in physical activity triggers the release of endorphins, neurotransmitters acting as natural stress relievers and mood enhancers. This surge of positivity not only leaves you elated post-workout but contributes to long-term mental well-being.

Craft a symphony of movement in your weekly routine, addressing various aspects of physical health. Attend a dance class to infuse joy and rhythm, embark on a refreshing morning jog to invigorate your senses, or embrace the tranquility of yoga for a holistic mind-body connection. The key is to discover activities resonating with your interests and lifestyle, transforming exercise from a routine task into a delightful and sustainable habit.

Rest and recovery are an often overlooked but critical component of your physical health. Allow your body sufficient time for repair through adequate sleep. Proper rest ensures muscle recovery, strengthens the immune system, and recharges the mind.

According to the Office of Population Affairs (n.d., para. 1): "Teenagers need at least 60 minutes of moderate to vigorous physical activity on most days to maintain good health and fitness and for healthy weight during growth." As you make choices about your health, healthy eating habits, including sufficient water intake and a diet rich in fruits and vegetables, become essential aspects of learning and adapting (Office of Population Affairs, n.d., para. 1).

According to Health.gov's Physical Activity Guidelines for Americans, the majority of adolescents' physical activity should involve heart-strengthening exercises, given their growing bodies (Office of Population Affairs, n.d.-a, para. 9).

Mental Well-being

Envision your mind as a lake, reflecting the clarity and calm that only deep, restful sleep can provide. Mental health takes center stage, and the conductor orchestrating this harmony is a night of rejuvenating sleep.

Adequate sleep is the cornerstone of mental well-being. Quality sleep isn't a luxury—it's a necessity for a vibrant mind. Plunging your body and mind into the restorative depths of sleep initiates a journey of mental rejuvenation.

During deep sleep, your brain consolidates memories, processes information, and enhances problem-solving skills. A well-rested mind is sharper, more focused, and better equipped to tackle the challenges of each day. It's the difference between a foggy morning and a clear, sunlit day.

Your mental landscape is a garden of emotions, and sleep is the nourishing rain that keeps it thriving. Sleep regulates mood, reducing irritability and promoting emotional stability. A good night's rest empowers you to face life's ups and downs with resilience, fostering a positive mindset and emotional well-being.

The immune system, your body's defender, relies on quality sleep to recharge its forces. Adequate rest enhances immune function, making you more resilient to illnesses and infections. The ripple effect of a well-supported immune system extends beyond physical health; it contributes to the overall balance of your mental well-being.

To unlock the full potential of your mental well-being, prioritize your sleep. Establish a calming bedtime routine signaling to your mind and body that it's time to unwind. Dim the lights to create a soothing ambiance, disconnect from screens to reduce exposure to stimulating light, and engage in relaxing activities like reading, gentle stretches, or calming music.

Aim for a consistent sleep schedule, allowing your body to synchronize with its natural circadian rhythms. This regularity improves sleep quality and reinforces your body's internal clock. Your mind thrives on routine, and a consistent sleep schedule helps support your mental well-being.

"Sleep is an important part of adolescents' health and well-being. Not getting adequate sleep at night can put adolescents at a higher risk for obesity, diabetes, poor mental health, and other problems" (Office of Population Affairs, n.d.-a, para. 15). The optimal amount of sleep for adolescents ages 13-18 is 8 to 10 hours, yet in 2019, less than a quarter of high school students reported getting the recommended eight hours on an average school night (Office of Population Affairs, n.d.-a, para. 15).

Fueling the Body and Mind: Nourishing Nutrition

Imagine your body as a high-performance vehicle, ready to hit the road at its peak. But here's the catch: to keep this machine running smoothly, it needs the right fuel. Your food and drink choices are the key players here. Put the wrong kind of fuel into your engine, and you'll feel the struggle. Once you figure out what makes your body tick, you'll experience your engine roaring to life!

Nutrition isn't just a side note; it's the foundation of well-being. From the energy pulsing through your veins to the clarity of your thoughts, the quality of your nutrition affects all aspects of your health—not just how your belly is filled.

Try your best to have both a balanced and varied diet. Make your plate a canvas waiting to be filled with colors. These power-packed fruits and vegetables are full of unique blends of vitamins, minerals, and antioxidants. Try to incorporate as many leafy greens, deep berries, and assorted vegetables as possible to infuse your diet with the nutrients it needs.

Power up your body with leaner proteins—the building blocks supporting muscle health and repair. Whether it's grilled chicken or tofu, lean proteins are filled with amino acids crucial for optimal bodily function. You can also introduce plant-based protein sources like legumes and quinoa to add diversity to your nutrient intake.

Be sure to include whole grains in your diet as well. Quinoa, brown rice, and oats aren't just staples; they're the sustenance providing a steady release of energy. Whole grains pack a punch with fiber, vitamins, and minerals, contributing to digestive health and sustained energy levels.

Do not be afraid of including healthy fats in your diet. Avocados, nuts, and seeds aren't just delicious; they're sources of omega-3 fatty acids and monounsaturated fats that promote cognitive function and heart health. Sprinkle nuts on your morning yogurt or indulge in avocado on whole-grain toast.

Along with nutrition, proper hydration completes your wellness picture. Water isn't just a beverage; it also aids digestion and nutrient absorption and regulates body temperature. Maintain a well-balanced diet that includes a variety of fruits, vegetables, lean proteins, whole grains, and healthy fats. Hydration and wholesome nutrition provide the fuel needed for optimal physical and mental performance.

Quoting insights from the Office of Population Affairs (n.d.-a), "Some adolescents may have more specific nutritional needs," and it's crucial to address these needs, especially considering factors like lower iron levels in adolescent girls compared to boys. The sources of iron mentioned include lean meats, poultry, seafood, legumes, dark-green leafy vegetables, and iron-enriched or fortified foods (para. 4). Additionally, barriers to accessing healthy food, such as living in food deserts or cost constraints, are recognized challenges that you could face (Office of Population Affairs, n.d.-a).

Balancing Act: Effective Stress Management

Life is filled with moments of joy, challenges that test us, and stress. Think of effective stress management as the art of finding balance against the ups and downs of life. Just like a skilled tightrope walker gracefully moves across the line, you, too, must learn to navigate the delicate balance between your dreams and the everyday demands life throws at you.

Stress is a natural response to life's challenges. It's like the kick of adrenaline that motivates you to overcome obstacles and reach your goals. However, just as too much spice can overpower a dish, when stress becomes chronic or overwhelming, it changes from a motivator to an adversary.

Imagine chronic stress as a relentless storm that, if left unchecked, can unravel and ultimately destroy your overall health. You must develop strategies that help you weather life's storms and fortify your resilience. Whether it's school pressures, personal challenges, or life's general hustle and bustle, having tools to manage stress becomes essential.

Stress is a part of life. It's not always bad; it can be a driving force pushing us toward success. Yet, being mindful of when stress becomes more than a motivator is critical. That's when you must employ the right strategies to keep your mental and physical well-being intact—just like a skilled tightrope walker gracefully maintaining balance on the thin line of life.

The Toll of Chronic Stress

Chronic stress has a profound impact on both your body and mind. Physically, it can manifest as tension, headaches, and compromised immune function. Mentally, it can lead to feelings of anxiety, irritability, and fatigue. Recognizing and proactively addressing the signs of stress is the first step toward creating a harmonious and resilient inner landscape.

By acknowledging and actively managing chronic stress, you start restoring the balance to your physical and mental well being. This self-awareness and proactive approach form the foundation for resilience, empowering you to navigate life's challenges with a steadier and more composed demeanor.

You may sometimes overlook signs of chronic stress or dismiss them as everyday aspects of daily life.

- **Physical symptoms**

    - **Frequent headaches:** Experiencing regular or persistent headaches, especially tension headaches, could be a physical manifestation of stress.

    - **Muscle tension:** Feeling tightness or tension in muscles, particularly in the neck, shoulders, or back, can indicate stress impacting the body.

- Sleep patterns

    - **Changes in sleep habits:** Insomnia, difficulty falling asleep, or irregular sleep patterns may indicate heightened stress levels.

    - **Fatigue:** Feeling persistently tired despite getting adequate sleep can result from chronic stress affecting overall energy levels.

- Emotional well-being

    - **Increased irritability:** Feeling more irritable or having a shorter fuse than usual might indicate emotional strain, especially in response to minor frustrations.

    - **Heightened anxiety***:*** Experiencing frequent worry, nervousness, or an overwhelming sense of unease can be indicative of chronic stress impacting mental well-being.

- Academic performance

    - **Difficulty concentrating:** Struggling to concentrate on tasks, assignments, or study material might suggest stress affects cognitive functions.

    - **Changes in grades***:*** A sudden decline in academic performance or changes in grades may be linked to stress affecting focus and motivation.

- Social behavior

    - **Withdrawal from activities:** Avoiding or withdrawing from activities that were once enjoyable or isolating oneself from friends might indicate emotional distress.

- **Increased agitation:** Becoming easily agitated, impatient, or having difficulty managing emotions in social situations can result from heightened stress.

- **Physical health**

  - **Frequent illness:** A compromised immune system due to stress may lead to an increased susceptibility to illnesses or a more extended recovery period.

  - **Digestive issues:** Stress can manifest in digestive problems such as stomachaches, nausea, or changes in appetite.

- **Self-care habits**

  - **Neglecting self-care:** Pay attention to changes in self-care habits, such as neglecting personal hygiene, grooming, or healthy eating, as these can indicate elevated stress levels.

It would be best if you recognized that experiencing occasional stress is normal, but when these signs become persistent or significantly impact daily life, it may indicate chronic stress. Seeking support from trusted friends, family members, or professionals is crucial in effectively managing stress and maintaining overall well-being.

Chapter 9:

Adaptability and Resilience

Life is a dynamic dance, a rhythm of changes and challenges that shape the narrative of your journey. Just as a skilled dancer adjusts their steps to the rhythm of a changing melody, you too must learn to adapt to the music of life and build the resilience needed to face its challenges.

Embracing Change

Embracing change is like leveling up in the game of life! Instead of worrying about change, let's flip the script and look at it like a chance to grow. Picture a tree swaying with the breeze instead of stubbornly standing still—being flexible in how you approach life boosts your ability to handle whatever comes your way. Every change, big or small, is like a secret level full of valuable lessons.

Adapting isn't just about going with the flow; it's about leveling up into a wiser and stronger you. Think of it as gaining experience points in the grand adventure of life. By learning from changes, you turn potential stress into a power-up for personal growth—a real game-changer.

Your teen years can be a wild river of emotions and transformations. In this crazy ride, being able to adapt isn't just a skill; it's your lifeboat, helping you handle the ups and downs of growth and self-discovery.

"Change can be tough, especially when it feels like you're saying goodbye to the old before saying hello to the new. It's like leveling up in a game, where you must leave the old challenges behind to conquer new ones. Even if it feels like a loss now, the victory ahead is worth it" (Getz, 2022, para. 3).

The Multifaceted Importance of Adaptability

Each challenge is an opportunity for personal growth. Academic pressures, evolving peer relationships, and the pursuit of self-identity shape a landscape where resilience stands as a coveted asset. Adaptability acts as a resilient shield, enabling you to rebound from setbacks and use those setbacks as stepping stones for personal development instead.

As you become more adaptable, you not only navigate the twists and turns of personal and academic challenges but approach them with a sense of creativity and resilience. Each problem becomes a puzzle, and adaptability becomes the key to unraveling it.

As Kovacs (2020, para. 2) aptly notes, "This ability to shift course is the fixed foundation upon which leaders build their lives. It's integral to successfully managing challenges as they come."

Furthermore, Kovacs (2020, para. 6) provides a valuable framework for self-reflection: "Trigger Event—What happened? Reference—How did you incorrectly evaluate the situation? Unhealthy Response—What did you do or say that you now regret? Truth—What was going on? Healthy Response—What can you do or say better the next time?"

Kirk (2022, para. 3) emphasizes the power of adaptability, stating, "An adaptable person can adjust their expectations quickly and move on to the new set circumstances without feeling anger, anxiety, or stress. Adaptable people can weather change without missing a beat. When people are adaptable, they can function—and even excel—when faced with situations that they can't predict or control.". Kirk (2022, para. 5) also highlights the interconnectedness of adaptability and resiliency: "Adaptability and resiliency go hand in hand. Children taught to be adaptable and resilient are empowered to take on life's many challenges to achieve their goals." Furthermore, in the classroom setting, teachers play a vital role in fostering adaptability by removing the stigma of failure. Kirk (2022, para. 12) suggests: "When thinking about adaptability in the classroom, teachers can help students learn to be adaptable by removing the stigma of failure. Students who are afraid of failure will turn away from trying new things. But trying new things and getting outside their comfort zone is key to developing adaptability skills. Also, failure can teach students to learn new ways of doing something, which teaches them how to overcome barriers."

Fostering Adaptability Through Practical Techniques

Goals give you a clear direction, while the built-in flexibility allows for adjustments.

Personal experiences are your origin tales—share them, especially the ones where positive outcomes emerged from challenging situations. These stories aren't just entertaining; they're like wisdom capsules, helping you see that change isn't just a disruption but a powerhouse for personal growth.

Time to broaden your horizons! Jump into different activities, explore diverse cultures, and discover unconventional experiences. This exposure becomes the ultimate adaptability tool, shaping an open-minded approach to change.

A strong support system is your personal superhero team. Foster open communication in your family, build connections with supportive friends, and seek guidance from mentors. This network is your safety net, ready to catch you and guide you when things get shaky.

Black Press Media (2023, para. 8): "By modeling adaptability, encouraging diverse experiences, teaching problem-solving skills, fostering independence, and emphasizing the importance of self-care, we can help our teenagers develop the skills they need to navigate the challenges of high school and beyond."

Adaptability In Real-World Applications

Consider actively looking for internships or volunteer opportunities! It's not just about gaining new skills; it's also a chance to learn how to adapt to different work settings and professional cultures. So, go ahead and explore different experiences—it's a great way to grow personally and professionally!

Champion the idea of travel experiences through school exchange programs or family vacations! Roaming around in unfamiliar places exposes you to different cultures and hones your adaptability skills by making you adjust to various customs and communication styles.

Let's talk about hands-on experiences—they stick with you. Get ready for decision-making challenges that make you think critically and be flexible. It's like a proactive boot camp for problem-solving skills and teaches you to adapt to real-world situations.

Understanding how to build a network is a super important life skill. Connecting with diverse groups opens you up to various perspectives and helps you be adaptable in both social and professional settings.

Are you facing academic challenges, like changing schools or adapting to different teaching styles? Seek support when needed; remember, these changes are a big part of your personal and intellectual growth.

In this age of crazy tech advancements, get into the groove of adaptability to emerging technologies. Dive into new software, learn digital tools, and stay on top of tech changes— it'll prep you for the ever-evolving tech scene.

Adaptability isn't about giving up on your goals but adjusting them based on changing circumstances. Understand this mindset shift and stay focused on your dreams while being flexible in reaching them.

Building emotional resilience is critical. Try exercises that boost emotional strength, like flipping negative thoughts into positive ones. It'll give you the mental toughness to tackle challenges positively and ease the emotional impact of change.

Social stuff is a big part of being adaptable. Dive into team-building activities that need collaboration and adaptation. These activities build teamwork and adaptability in different social scenes, whether at school, in sports, or with your community crew.

Life simulation games or scenarios are like real-world challenges in a controlled environment. It's an engaging way to prepare you for whatever the future throws!

Building Resilience in the Face of Adversity

Resilience is our protective armor, shielding us when life throws challenges our way. It's not about dodging difficulties but about fostering inner strength to face them head-on and emerge even stronger on the other side.

But guess what? Resilience isn't an exclusive trait for a chosen few; it's a skill we can intentionally develop.

Now, picture a growth mindset where resilience takes root and flourishes. We'll explore how embracing challenges as growth opportunities can shift our perspective. By viewing setbacks as stepping stones toward success, we lay the foundation for a resilient mindset that can weather life's storms.

And here's the deal: self-care isn't a luxury—it's a necessity for building resilience. Things like getting enough sleep, eating properly, and establishing healthy boundaries with others, among others, are important pieces in your resilience toolkit.

Building resilience is not about avoiding difficulties but about intentionally developing the inner strength to confront them head-on and emerge stronger on the other side.

Tomás-Keegan (2020, para. 21): "Even the most resilient people need time to adjust to the new reality when a major life event occurs. They may need time to recover from an injury, go through the grieving process, or start thinking more clearly again" (para. 15). And remember, "When you adjust your perspective, you can see things from another angle. You can see opportunities where there were obstacles."

Tomás-Keegan (2020) suggests a powerful reframing tool: "Ask yourself: What can I learn from this? What are my options? These questions turn you away from the blame game and allow you to focus on the good that might come from the situation" (para. 22). Gratitude, as noted by Tomás-Keegan, is a potent tool: "Search for small things you can be grateful for" (para. 33).

Think about school and balancing time for yourself and your friends—it can get intense. This is where resilience plays a crucial role. It's your secret weapon, helping you bounce back from setbacks, whether it's a challenging exam or a rocky patch in your social circles. It's like having this mental superpower that gives you the strength to power through the tough times and come out the other side stronger.

Life is full of twists and turns. Resilience teaches you how to navigate and adapt to these changes. It's like having a mental GPS that helps you find your way when things get tricky. This adaptive thinking becomes your guide, not just in school but in all areas of life.

Resilience is about building emotional strength—understanding your feelings, handling stress, and finding ways to stay positive even when things get tough. This emotional fortitude becomes your armor against the challenges that come your way. Tomás-Keegan (2020): "A strong body and mind are key elements when it comes to building resilience in the face of adversity" (para. 34). And here's a fun twist: "Finding the funny in adversity can lighten the load we carry when bad stuff happens" (para. 41).

Resilience isn't about giving up; it's about pushing through. When things get challenging, resilience gives you the perseverance to keep going. It's like having a built-in cheerleader, encouraging you to tackle difficulties head-on and come out on top.

The skills you develop through resilience aren't just for now; they set the stage for your future success. You're building a toolkit of life skills that will serve you well.

Self-care is like a tag team for your mind and body. Taking care of your physical well-being—getting enough sleep, eating nutritious meals, and staying active—directly impacts your mental health. It's the fuel that powers your resilience engine.

Adolescence is a time of intense emotions, and letting yourself feel all the feelings is more than okay. Self-care involves checking in with your feelings regularly. Whether journaling, talking to a friend, or practicing positive thinking, finding healthy outlets for your feelings strengthens your emotional resilience.

Resilience means taking on the world only in stages. It's about setting boundaries. Know when to say no and when to prioritize your own needs. Establishing healthy boundaries helps you conserve energy and balance your responsibilities and self-care.

Resilience thrives in a supportive environment. Build connections with friends, family, or mentors who uplift and understand you. Sharing your experiences and seeking support strengthens your social resilience, providing a safety net during challenging times.

Among the hustle and bustle of life, give yourself the gift of relaxation. Find activities that bring you peace, whether reading a book, listening to music, or practicing deep breathing exercises. Learning to relax is a key component of self-care that rejuvenates your mind and body.

Resilience isn't just about bouncing back from setbacks and acknowledging your victories. Celebrate the small wins—whether it's acing a quiz, completing a project, or simply getting through a tough day. Recognizing your achievements fuels a positive mindset and reinforces your ability to overcome challenges.

Self-care includes making time for things you love. Engage in hobbies and activities that bring you joy and fulfillment. Whether playing a musical instrument, drawing, or a sport, these pursuits act as a refreshing break, contributing to your overall well-being.

Sometimes, self-care involves recognizing when you need extra support. If you find yourself struggling with overwhelming stress or emotional challenges, don't hesitate to seek guidance from a counselor, therapist, or a trusted adult. Seeking professional support is a proactive step toward building resilience.

Remember, self-care isn't a luxury; it's a necessity. It's the foundation that supports your resilience, helping you navigate the twists and turns of adolescence with strength and grace. So, prioritize yourself, take time for self-care, and watch how it transforms your ability to conquer challenges and emerge even more resilient.

Chapter 10:

Cooking Skills

Cooking is about unleashing your creativity, exploring diverse flavors, and turning your kitchen into a playground of possibilities.

Kitchen Fundamentals

The Essential Knives: Your Kitchen Allies

In the heart of your kitchen, indispensable tools are waiting to become your trusted companions—knives.

Chef's Knife: All-Purpose Precision

The Chef's Knife is your kitchen workhorse. Its broad and sturdy blade, often between six to ten inches, makes it ideal for chopping, dicing, and slicing with precision. Consider it your go-to tool for kitchen tasks, making meal preparation a breeze.

Paring Knife: Precision in Small Packages

When finesse is required, the paring knife steps up to the plate. With a smaller and more maneuverable blade, typically three to four inches, it is perfect for tasks like peeling fruits, deveining shrimp, or any job demanding precision. Its pointed tip allows for intricate movements, making it the agile companion for delicate maneuvers in the kitchen.

Utility Knife: The Versatile Assistant

The utility knife bridges the gap between the chef's and paring knives. Ideal for slicing sandwiches, cheese, or smaller fruits, it's a versatile companion with the flexibility to handle various cutting needs. The utility knife is your go-to for everyday kitchen tasks, from slicing through cheeses to fruit cuts.

Serrated Bread Knife: Crust Conqueror

The serrated bread knife is your ally for crusty loaves, bagels, and tomatoes. Its serrated edge allows it to effortlessly slice through tough exteriors without crushing delicate interiors. It is an essential addition to your kitchen arsenal, a powerful tool for achieving clean and precise cuts.

Knife Handling Tips for Young Chefs

- **Grip it right:** Hold the knife with a firm but comfortable grip. Place your index finger and thumb on opposite sides of the blade's base, forming a secure pinch grip. This provides stability and control while cutting.

- **Practice safe techniques:** Master proper cutting techniques, such as the chef's knife's rocking motion and the paring knife's precision grip. Always curl your fingertips inward to avoid accidents and ensure safe-cutting practices.

- **Keep it sharp:** A sharp knife is safer than a dull one. Regularly hone and sharpen your knives to maintain their effectiveness and reduce the risk of accidents. Worn blades can slip, increasing the likelihood of injuries.

- **Respect the blade:** Treat knives with respect. Avoid using them on hard surfaces like glass or ceramic, as it can damage the blade. Always clean and store knives properly to maintain their sharpness and longevity.

- **Learn knife skills:** Embrace the learning process and gradually build your expertise in cutting techniques. Knife skills are essential for becoming a proficient chef, and consistent practice enhances your proficiency.

Why Learning Knife Skills is Important for Young Chefs

- **Safety first:** Proper knife skills reduce the risk of accidents in the kitchen, ensuring your safety and the safety of those around you. Understanding how to handle knives safely is a fundamental aspect of responsible cooking.

- **Efficiency and precision:** Mastering knife skills enhance your efficiency in the kitchen. You can tackle tasks precisely, resulting in well-prepared ingredients and more enjoyable cooking experiences.

- **Culinary confidence:** Your culinary confidence grows as you become adept with knives. You'll approach cooking with newfound assurance, allowing your creativity to flourish. Confidence in using knives enables you to experiment with different cooking techniques and recipes.

- **Professionalism:** Developing knife skills is a hallmark of culinary professionalism. Whether you aspire to be a chef or enjoy cooking at home, these skills elevate your culinary prowess.

- **Appreciation for ingredients:** Understanding how to handle ingredients with knives properly allows you to appreciate the textures and flavors of each element in your dish.

Cutting Boards

Cutting boards provide a stable surface for chopping, slicing, and preparing ingredients. Despite their critical role, they are often overshadowed by more impressive kitchen gadgets.

Whether you opt for the natural elegance of wood or the practicality of plastic, your cutting board is a loyal companion, ensuring each slice and chop is a step toward a delicious masterpiece. So, give your cutting board the recognition it deserves.

Here's why they deserve your attention:

- **Knife and ingredient protection:** Cutting boards shield your knives, preventing them from dulling prematurely. They also protect your countertop from scratches and nicks caused by sharp blades.

- **Food safety assurance:** Properly chosen and maintained cutting boards contribute to a hygienic kitchen environment by preventing cross-contamination. Using separate boards for different food types, such as meats and vegetables, ensures the safety of your meals.

- **Preventing bacterial growth:** Cutting boards have natural antimicrobial properties that inhibit the growth of bacteria. This makes them a safe and reliable surface for food preparation.

- **Versatility and durability:** Available in various materials, cutting boards cater to different culinary needs. From the elegance of wooden boards to the practicality of plastic ones, they offer versatility and durability for diverse kitchen tasks.

Types of Cutting Boards

- **Wooden cutting board**: Wooden cutting boards are an aesthetic addition to your kitchen. They are gentle on your knives, preserving their sharpness and adding a touch of natural elegance to your culinary space. Ideal for slicing fruits and vegetables, these boards are functional and visually appealing.

- **Plastic cutting board:** Plastic cutting boards are the go-to for handling raw meats. Easy to clean and maintain, they provide a dedicated space for cutting proteins. Color-coded options help prevent cross-contamination, with designated boards for different food groups ensuring a safe and sanitary culinary environment.

Safety Protocols for Cutting Boards

- **Separate boards for different foods:** Use respective cutting boards for raw meats, vegetables, fruits, and other food categories. This prevents cross-contamination and ensures the safety of your meals.

- **Regular cleaning and sanitizing:** Clean cutting boards thoroughly after each use. For plastic boards, they can often be sanitized in the dishwasher. Wooden boards should be cleaned with mild soap and warm water.

- **Avoiding deep cuts and scratches:** Deep cuts and scratches in cutting boards can harbor bacteria. Regularly inspect your boards for any signs of wear and replace them if needed.

- **Proper storage:** Store cutting boards in a dry and well-ventilated area to prevent moisture buildup, which can lead to bacterial growth. Avoid stacking damp boards to ensure they remain in optimal condition.

- **Material-specific care:** Follow care instructions specific to the material of your cutting board. For example, wooden boards may require occasional oiling to maintain their integrity.

Reliable Kitchen Tools

Other tools will be handy to have in your arsenal.

Spatulas

- **Turner spatula:** The turner spatula is perfect for flipping pancakes, burgers, or delicate items like fish fillets. Its thin, flat edge effortlessly slides under the food.

- **Rubber spatula:** The rubber spatula ensures no batter or sauce is left behind in the bowl. It is perfect for folding ingredients gently, scraping bowl sides, and achieving uniform mixtures.

- **Offset spatula:** The offset spatula is ideal for spreading frosting, smoothing batter, or lifting delicate items; its offset handle provides excellent control.

Whisks

- **Balloon whisk:** The balloon whisk is designed for beating air into batters, whipping cream, and creating fluffy eggs. Its rounded shape ensures thorough mixing and aeration.

- **Flat whisk:** Ideal for sauces and gravies, the flat whisk's shape reaches the edges of pans, ensuring smooth, lump-free results—achieving silky textures.

Trusty Mixing Bowls

- **Large mixing bowl:** This is perfect for extensive dough, salads, or marinating protein batches. Its generous size accommodates thorough mixing and tossing for family-sized meals.

- **Medium mixing bowl:** This bowl is an all-purpose companion for mixing ingredients and tossing salads. Its midsize offers versatility in various culinary tasks, making it an essential part of your kitchen ensemble.

- **Small mixing bowl:** The small mixing bowl is ideal for precise measurements and whisking smaller quantities. Perfect for creating sauces, dressings, or smaller recipe batches with precision.

Mixing Bowl Tips

- **Nested organization:** Nest mixing bowls for efficient storage, optimizing your kitchen space.

- **Material matters:** Choose mixing bowls made of durable materials that withstand the demands of your cooking.

- **Versatile vessels:** Utilize mixing bowls for mixing, serving, and presenting dishes with flair.

Measuring Tools

- **Liquid measuring cup:** The liquid measuring cup, designed for liquids, ensures accurate measurements with its spout for easy pouring. Measure at eye level to guarantee precision in your liquids.

- **Dry measuring cups:** Ideal for ingredients like flour and sugar, dry measuring cups come in various sizes for versatility.

- **Measuring spoons:** Measuring spoons are reliable for precise seasoning, whether a dash or a pinch. Ensure accuracy in smaller quantities of spices and extracts.

Measurement Magic—Cooking Measurements and Conversions

Like a skilled artisan using tools, mastering the nuances of precise measurements is your gateway to culinary excellence. Whether you're an experienced chef or an eager home cook, delving into the intricacies of cooking measurements opens up a realm of possibilities.

Teaspoons and Tablespoons

Consider teaspoons and tablespoons as fundamental tools in your culinary toolkit, serving as precision instruments that enhance your cooking expertise. With the teaspoon and tablespoon at your disposal, you can ensure that every dish is perfectly balanced, with flavors seamlessly intertwined for a delightful dining experience.

Visualize the teaspoon as your compact yet influential tool, designed for delicately infusing a hint of spice or a subtle flavor boost to your dishes. It is the conductor of precise seasoning, enabling you to elevate your culinary creations with a nuanced touch for a well-balanced taste.

See the tablespoon as your larger, impactful tool, capable of delivering more substantial bursts of flavor. Whether a tablespoon of aromatic herbs or a drizzle of flavorful oil, this robust instrument adds bold and pronounced taste elements to your dishes.

Measuring Cups

Cups are essential in your kitchen, holding the secret to impeccable measurements. Different cup sizes empower you to navigate a spectrum of quantities, ensuring that your dishes consistently deliver the intended flavors and textures. Cup measurements provide the reliability needed for crafting exceptional recipes, making them an indispensable aspect of your culinary toolkit.

1-Cup Measuring Cup

The 1-cup measuring cup becomes your trusted ally for larger quantities. Whether flour, liquids, or grains, this cup ensures that your recipes consistently achieve the perfect volume, allowing you to create culinary masterpieces confidently.

1/2-Cup and 1/4-Cup Measuring Cups

Precision is paramount when dealing with smaller amounts, and the 1/2-cup and 1/4-cup measuring cups step in for this purpose. These cups are indispensable for achieving the ideal balance in your recipes, especially when working with concentrated or potent ingredients.

The Art of Effortlessly Converting Ingredients

Mastering these conversion skills is akin to unlocking the door to culinary versatility. It allows you to seamlessly navigate different measurements, ensuring that your culinary creations consistently hit the right notes. With these conversion techniques at your fingertips, you gain the confidence to tailor recipes to your preferences while maintaining the precision that defines exceptional cooking.

- **1 tablespoon (tbsp) = 3 teaspoons (tsp):** Precision is vital for seasoning adjustments. If a recipe specifies tablespoons, but you prefer using teaspoons, this conversion ensures that your seasoning remains spot-on. It provides the flexibility to adapt recipes to your taste preferences without compromising accuracy.

- **1 cup (c) = 16 tablespoons (tbsp):** The need to scale up or down in the kitchen is shared. Whether adjusting a recipe's quantity or dealing with various measuring tools, converting 1 cup to 16 tablespoons is a reliable guide. This conversion ensures that your portions stay accurate, regardless of your adjustments.

Cooking Techniques

It's time to unveil your cooking skills and become the kitchen hero you were always meant to be. Whether you're boiling, sautéing, baking, or grilling, these techniques are vital to creating delicious meals.

Boiling Basics

Embracing boiling is like mastering a fundamental process that turns raw ingredients into tender delights.

Mastering the Art of Boiling

- **Water fundamentals:** Elevate the taste by adding a pinch of salt, enhancing the flavors by infusing your ingredients. The goal is to bring the water to a rolling boil.

- **Ingredient integration:** With the water bubbling and ready, delicately introduce your chosen ingredients. Whether it's pasta, vegetables, or grains, the boiling process allows these components to absorb flavors while achieving the desired tenderness.

- **Precision in timing:** In the world of boiling, timing is crucial. Utilize timers or adhere to recommended timings to ensure culinary perfection. Overboiling risks turning your ingredients mushy, while undercooking leaves them firm and raw. Achieving the ideal tenderness requires precision, and the timing aspect is your compass to navigate this culinary journey successfully.

- **Culinary infusion:** Boiling transcends mere cooking; it's an opportunity to infuse your ingredients with various flavors. Take your culinary creations to the next level by experimenting with different broths, herbs, and spices. This infusion process adds layers of depth, transforming your boiled dishes into culinary dishes that awaken your taste buds.

Elevate Your Boiling Experience

- **Broth:** Explore a variety of broths—from vegetable and chicken to beef or seafood.

- **Herbs and spices:** Elevate the flavor profile by experimenting with herbs and spices.

- **Citrus zest and zing:** Add a burst of freshness with citrus zest. Lemon, lime, or orange zest introduces a zing that brightens up your boiled dishes, offering a delightful contrast to the savory notes.

- **Bold broil:** Consider briefly broiling or roasting certain ingredients before introducing them to the boiling pot. This technique enhances flavors, providing a nuanced depth that distinguishes culinary creations.

Boiling becomes a culinary journey where precision, timing, and creativity converge. It's not just about cooking; it's about crafting masterpieces that delight the senses. With this comprehensive guide, you're poised to elevate your boiling experience, transforming simple ingredients into culinary marvels that showcase your expertise in the kitchen.

Sautéing

Embrace the culinary finesse of sautéing, a dynamic interplay of ingredients in a heated pan orchestrating a symphony of flavors.

Mastering the Technique of Sautéing:

- **Pan mastery:** Initiate the sautéing process by heating a pan with a subtle amount of oil or butter. Allow it to reach an optimal temperature, ensuring it's adequately heated without producing smoke.

- **Ingredient choreography:** With the pan ready, introduce your finely chopped vegetables, proteins, or aromatics into the mix. Engage in swift, controlled movements as you stir-fry, ensuring each element receives equal attention.

- **Fusion of flavors:** Sautéing is a technique that transcends mere cooking; it's a flavor fusion extravaganza. This method melts the ingredients' flavors, creating a harmonious union.

Your Path to Culinary Creativity

Sautéing is more than a cooking method; it's your passport to a world of vibrant flavors and textures. Seize the opportunity to experiment with various oils, herbs, and spices to craft your signature sautéed masterpieces.

- **Flavorful oils:** Venture into the world of delicious oils like olive, sesame, or infused oils to impart distinct notes to your sautéed creations.

- **Herbs and spices:** Elevate the flavor profile with herbs and spices. From the warmth of thyme to the kick of paprika, these additions turn your sautéed dishes into culinary masterpieces.

- **Citrus zest elevation:** Add a burst of freshness with citrus zest. Lemon or orange zest introduces a zing that brightens your sautéed dishes, creating a delightful contrast to the savory notes.

- **Nutty indulgence:** Experiment with nutty oils or incorporate toasted nuts for an indulgent touch, providing a delightful crunch and a layer of richness to your sautéed creations.

Baking

Baking is the systematic transformation of raw mixtures into golden delights.

Time to unlock the secrets:

- **Precise potions:** Preheat your oven to the temperature specified in your recipe. Gather your ingredients—flour, sugar, eggs, and more.

- **Mixture magic:** Combine your ingredients, creating a batter or dough.

- **Oven mastery**: Place your creation in the preheated oven. Watch as the magic unfolds—the rise, the browning, the delightful aromas.

- **Patience pays off:** Baking requires patience. Follow the suggested baking time, and you'll be rewarded with delectable treats.

Baking is about following recipes and experimenting with flavors, textures, and aromas. Add different extracts, fruits, or nuts to create your baked wonders.

Mastering Grilling

- **Fire preparation:** Initiate the grilling process by preheating your grill to the desired temperature. Allow the flames to work their magic, creating an environment where food meets fire in a dance that elevates the taste and texture of your dishes.

- **Marination method:** Enhance the flavor profile of your proteins or veggies by immersing them in a marination bath. This step adds depth and complexity to your grilled creations. Before placing them on the grill, brush the marinated items with oil to prevent sticking and ensure a perfect sear.

- **Grill charisma:** Place your marinated items on the grill grates. The following sizzle and char will awaken your taste buds, creating a symphony of aromas that captivate the senses. The grill becomes your stage, and each item a performer, delivering a culinary spectacle of flavors.

- **Flipping finesse:** Achieve grilling perfection using tongs for a flawless flip. Grill marks and a smoky essence are not just signs of successful grilling; they represent the artistry of the process. Mastering the flip ensures even cooking and that coveted balance of char and tenderness.

Grilling as a Sensory Experience:

Grilling transcends mere cooking, a sensory experience that engages sight, smell, and taste. Elevate your grilling by experimenting with different marinades, wood chips, and techniques.

- **Marinade exploration:** Dive into the world of marinades, exploring combinations of herbs, spices, oils, and acids. Each marination adds a unique touch to your grilled masterpiece, whether a savory soy-based blend or a zesty citrus infusions.

- **Wood chip adventure:** Elevate your grilling by experimenting with different wood chips. Each wood type imparts distinct flavors, from hickory and mesquite to applewood and cherry, allowing you to tailor your grilled creations to your taste preferences.

- **Grilling techniques:** Expand your grilling repertoire by exploring various techniques. Each method offers a different dimension to your culinary creations, from direct grilling for quick searing to indirect grilling for slow cooking.

Exploring Different Food Prep Methods

Now that you've mastered the basics, it's time to move on to more complicated methods. Beyond boiling, sautéing, baking, and grilling, a universe of food prep methods is waiting to be discovered. Each technique is a portal to new flavors and textures.

Roasting

Embark on the culinary journey of roasting, a pathway to intensified flavors and the allure of caramelized goodness.

- **Oven adventure:** Begin roasting by preheating your oven to a high temperature. This initial step is crucial, creating the perfect environment for a beautiful sear that locks in the natural juices of your ingredients.

- **Seasoning sophistication:** Elevate your ingredients with a touch of seasoning savvy. Envelop them in a symphony of herbs, spices, and a drizzle of oil, ensuring each element is bathed in flavorful goodness.

- **Golden transformation:** Roast your seasoned ingredients until a golden exterior and succulent interior are achieved.

Steaming Styles

Steaming is the gentle caress of hot steam, preserving nutrients and creating tender bites. Steaming is more than a cooking method; it's the art of maintaining freshness and nutrients. Dive into steaming with an adventurous spirit, exploring different combinations of herbs, spices, and aromatics to infuse your ingredients with delightful aromas.

- **Steam setup:** Initiate your steaming expedition by selecting the appropriate steaming apparatus. Whether it's a traditional bamboo steamer, a modern electric steamer, or a simple pot with a well-fitted basket, the key is to create a conducive environment for the magic of steam to work on your ingredients.

- **Aromatic infusions:** Elevate your steaming experience by introducing aromatic additions. Infuse your ingredients with the essence of herbs, citrus, or other aromatics that complement the dish. This step transforms steaming into a sensory journey, where the aroma becomes integral to the culinary symphony.

- **Steam symphony:** Allow the steam to perform its symphony until your vegetables or proteins reach the pinnacle of tenderness. This method retains the natural colors of your ingredients and ensures that the nutritional value remains intact. The result is a harmonious blend of textures and flavors, where each bite is a testament to the delicate touch of steam.

Braising Adventures

Braising is the slow-cooking embrace of moist heat, resulting in melt-in-your-mouth textures. Immerse yourself in the creative process by experimenting with various braising liquids, aromatics, and complementary ingredients to craft your signature braised delights.

- **Sear strategy:** Initiate the braising process by employing a sear strategy. Sear your ingredients in a hot pan, creating a caramelized exterior that locks in the inherent flavors. This initial step sets the stage for a depth of taste that will unfold during the slow-cooking embrace.

- **Liquid layers:** Introduce a layer of complexity by adding a flavorful liquid to the seared ingredients. Whether broth, wine, or a blend of aromatic liquids, this step provides a foundation for slow cooking and infuses your dish with nuanced tastes that develop over time.

- **Low-and-slow simmer:** Engage in the slow dance of braising as you allow your ingredients to simmer gently in the flavorful liquid. The low-and-slow simmer is the alchemy behind achieving heavenly textures. This method transforms tough cuts of meat and sturdy vegetables into tender goodness, creating a symphony of flavors that harmonize every bite.

Searing Styles

Take on the culinary adventure of searing, a high-heat embrace that crafts a golden crust, sealing in the succulent juices of your ingredients.

- **Hot surface setup:** Heat a pan or skillet to a high temperature, creating the perfect stage for the sizzling sear. This crucial step sets the foundation for the transformative process that follows.

- **Oil application:** Enhance the searing experience by delicately brushing your ingredients with oil. This thoughtful application facilitates the burning process and adds a layer of richness to the final result. The oil becomes a conductor, orchestrating the symphony of flavors unfolding in the hot pan.

- **Sizzle symphony:** Witness the crescendo of flavor as you place your oil-brushed items onto the hot pan. Listen attentively for the sizzle—the sound of flavor locking in, juices searing, and a golden crust forming.

Stir-Frying

Stir-frying is the high-energy dance of ingredients in a hot wok or pan.

- **Wok work:** Kickstart your stir-fry by preparing your wok or pan and heating it to a sizzling high temperature. Stir-frying is a rapid cooking technique, and the work serves as the stage for this high-energy culinary dance. The searing heat is the key to achieving the perfect stir-fry texture and flavor.

- **Ingredient integration:** Engage in the lively choreography of stir-frying by adding your meticulously sliced veggies, proteins, and aromatic companions to the hot wok. Toss and stir with swift, controlled movements, ensuring that each element is kissed by the intense heat, resulting in a symphony of textures and tastes that dance on your palate.

- **Sauce symphony:** Elevate your stir-fry creation by introducing different sauces. Whether it's a savory soy-based sauce, a zesty teriyaki blend, or a fiery chili-infused concoction, adding flavorful sauces or seasonings transforms your stir-fry. Each ingredient absorbs the essence, contributing to the depth and complexity of the final masterpiece.

Meal Planning and Nutrition

Imagine your meal as a well-curated playlist with a mix of your favorite tunes. In the world of food, it's about creating a balanced composition. Include proteins like chicken or beans, carbs such as whole grains, healthy fats like avocados, and a burst of color from various fruits and veggies. This way, every meal becomes a nutrient-packed melody for your body.

Just like selecting the right volume for your music, keeping an eye on portion sizes is crucial. Smaller plates are like choosing the right speakers—they create an illusion of abundance without overwhelming you. It's about enjoying the perfect serving size for a satisfying meal.

Think of snacks as your favorite tunes between the main acts. Fresh fruits, nuts, or yogurt are like the upbeat interludes that keep your energy levels high without missing a beat. They add a delightful note to your culinary narrative.

Water is your backstage hero, ensuring everything runs smoothly. Just as a concert needs a well-hydrated orchestra, your body needs water for optimum performance. Make a conscious effort to include ample water throughout your daily routine—it's the secret ingredient to a well-hydrated body.

Get Creative in the Kitchen

Your kitchen is your stage, and the ingredients are your instruments. Experiment with different flavors, spices, and herbs to create a symphony of tastes. Let your creativity flow, Whether trying out a new cuisine or infusing unique ingredients. Cooking becomes a delightful exploration of culinary possibilities.

Your palate is an adventure map with different ingredients, like exciting destinations. Explore a variety of tastes and textures by incorporating a mix of savory and sweet, spicy and mild. Each meal becomes a journey through diverse culinary landscapes.

Culinary Tips

- **Theme nights:** Designate specific nights for culinary themes—it's like hosting a mini-food festival in your kitchen. "Mediterranean Monday" or "Taco Tuesday" adds an element of excitement to your meal plan.

- **Try new ingredients:** Keep the excitement alive by regularly introducing new ingredients. It's like discovering new flavors that add a dash of surprise to your meals. Whether it's a unique spice or an exotic vegetable, let your taste buds go on new adventures

- **Experiment with cooking:** Your kitchen is a laboratory, and cooking techniques are your experiments. Try grilling, roasting, or steaming to bring different textures and flavors to your meals. It's about adding layers of complexity to your culinary creations.

- **Go seasonal:** Seasonal produce is like nature's gift to your kitchen. It adds freshness and variety to your meals and connects you with the changing seasons. From crisp apples in fall to juicy berries in summer, embrace nature's seasonal surprises.

So, in this culinary journey, you're not just a chef—you're a maestro crafting a masterpiece of flavors. Enjoy the process, let your creativity flow, and may every meal be a unique composition that resonates with your taste buds and nourishes your well-being. Bon appétit!

Meal Plan

Day One

- **Breakfast:** Greek yogurt parfait with fresh berries and granola

- **Lunch:** grilled chicken salad with mixed greens, cherry tomatoes, cucumbers, and balsamic vinaigrette

- **Dinner:** baked salmon with lemon-dill sauce, quinoa, and steamed broccoli

Day Two

- **Breakfast:** whole grain toast with avocado and poached egg
- **Lunch:** chickpea salad with mixed vegetables and feta cheese
- **Dinner:** stir-fried tofu with vegetables (bell peppers, broccoli, snap peas) and brown rice

Day Three

- **Breakfast:** smoothie with spinach, banana, frozen berries, Greek yogurt, and almond milk
- **Lunch:** turkey and hummus wrap with whole wheat tortilla, lettuce, and tomatoes
- **Dinner:** spaghetti with marinara sauce and a side salad

Day 4

- **Breakfast:** oatmeal with sliced banana, almonds, and a drizzle of honey
- **Lunch:** quinoa bowl with black beans, corn, avocado, and salsa
- **Dinner:** grilled chicken breast with sweet potato fries and roasted Brussels sprouts

Some Beginner Friendly Recipes

Grilled Chicken Salad

Ingredients:

- one boneless, skinless chicken breast
- mixed salad greens (lettuce, spinach, arugula)
- cherry tomatoes, halved
- cucumber, sliced
- red onion, thinly sliced
- balsamic vinaigrette dressing

Instructions:

1. Season the chicken breast with salt, pepper, and olive oil.
2. Grill the chicken on medium-high heat for 6-8 minutes per side or until fully cooked.
3. Combine the salad greens, cherry tomatoes, cucumber, and red onion in a large bowl.
4. Slice the grilled chicken and place it on top of the salad.
5. Drizzle the balsamic vinaigrette dressing over the salad.
6. Toss everything together to combine the flavors.

This meal plan and recipe provide a good balance of protein, carbohydrates, healthy fats, and various vitamins and minerals. Feel free to adjust portions based on your individual needs, and don't hesitate to explore different ingredients and cooking methods as you become more comfortable with meal planning.

Grilled Lemon Herb Salmon with Braised Vegetables

Ingredients

For Grilled Lemon Herb Salmon:

- 2 salmon fillets
- 2 tablespoons olive oil
- 1 lemon (zested and juiced)
- 2 cloves garlic, minced
- 1 teaspoon dried thyme
- 1 teaspoon dried rosemary
- salt and pepper to taste

For Braised Vegetables:

- 1 zucchini, sliced
- 1 red bell pepper, sliced
- 1 yellow bell pepper, sliced
- 1 cup cherry tomatoes, halved

- 1 onion, thinly sliced
- 2 tablespoons balsamic vinegar
- 2 tablespoons soy sauce
- 1 tablespoon honey
- 2 tablespoons olive oil
- salt and pepper to taste

Optional

- quinoa or couscous for serving

Instructions:

1. Mix olive oil, lemon zest, lemon juice, minced garlic, dried thyme, rosemary, salt, and pepper in a bowl to create a marinade.

2. Place the salmon fillets in a shallow dish, pour the marinade over them, and let them marinate in the refrigerator for at least 30 minutes.

3. Preheat your grill to medium heat.

4. In a large skillet, heat olive oil over medium heat. Add sliced zucchini, red and yellow bell peppers, cherry tomatoes, and onion.

5. Mix balsamic vinegar, soy sauce, honey, salt, and pepper in a small bowl. Pour this mixture over the vegetables.

6. Braise the vegetables for about 10-12 minutes or until they are tender but still vibrant, stirring occasionally.

7. Remove the salmon from the marinade and place the fillets on the preheated grill. Grill for approximately 4-5 minutes per side or until the salmon is cooked to your desired doneness.

8. Arrange the grilled lemon herb salmon on a plate alongside the braised vegetables.

9. Optionally, serve over a bed of quinoa or couscous to absorb the flavorful juices.

10. Enjoy!

Tips

- Adjust grilling times based on the thickness of the salmon fillets.

- Experiment with additional herbs or spices in the salmon marinade to suit your taste preferences.

- Don't be afraid to get creative with the braised vegetables – try adding mushrooms or asparagus for extra variety.

Chocolate Chip Cookies

Ingredients:

- 1 cup (2 sticks) unsalted butter, softened
- 1 cup granulated sugar
- 1 cup packed brown sugar
- 2 large eggs
- 1 teaspoon vanilla extract

- 3 cups all-purpose flour
- 1 teaspoon baking soda
- 1/2 teaspoon baking powder
- 1/2 teaspoon salt
- 2 cups chocolate chips

Instructions:

1. Preheat your oven to 350 °F (180 °C)—line two baking sheets with parchment paper.

2. In a large mixing bowl, cream the softened butter, granulated sugar, and brown sugar until the mixture is light and fluffy. This can be done with a hand mixer or stand mixer.

3. Add the eggs one at a time, beating well after each addition. Then, mix in the vanilla extract until well combined.

4. Whisk together the all-purpose flour, baking soda, baking powder, and salt in a separate bowl.

5. Gradually add the dry ingredients to the wet ingredients, mixing until combined. Be careful not to overmix; this ensures your cookies stay tender.

6. Gently fold in the chocolate chips using a spatula or wooden spoon until evenly distributed throughout the cookie dough.

7. Using a cookie scoop or tablespoon, drop rounded portions of dough onto the prepared baking sheets, leaving enough space between each cookie.

8. Bake in the oven for 10-12 minutes or until the edges are golden brown. The center may look slightly underbaked but will continue to set as the cookies cool.

9. Allow the cookies to cool on the baking sheets for a few minutes before transferring them to a wire rack to cool completely. This step is essential for achieving that perfect chewy texture.

Tips

- Ensure your butter is softened but not melted for the best texture.

- Use room-temperature eggs for better incorporation into the dough.

- Please don't skip letting the cookies cool on the baking sheets; it helps them set without becoming too crisp.

Understanding Dietary Needs

Become a dietary detective as we uncover the mysteries of different nutritional needs. Whether you're a vegetarian or just exploring healthy choices, there are plenty of options to make meals that cater to everyone's preferences.

Vegetarian Ventures

For those embracing a vegetarian lifestyle, the focus is on plant-based goodness.

- **Protein picks:** Incorporate plant-based protein sources like beans, lentils, tofu, and tempeh. These add protein and bring unique flavors and textures to your meals.

- **Colorful crusade:** Load your plate with various colorful vegetables and fruits. This ensures a diverse range of vitamins, minerals, and antioxidants.

- **Whole grain wonders:** Choose whole grains like quinoa, brown rice, and oats to provide essential carbohydrates and fiber for sustained energy.

Protein Prowess

- **Lean options:** Opt for lean protein sources like chicken, turkey, fish, eggs, and lean cuts of beef or pork. These provide high-quality protein with less saturated fat.

- **Balanced plates:** Combine protein with vegetables, whole grains, and healthy fats for a well-rounded and satisfying meal.

- **Plant-powered protein:** Don't forget plant-based protein sources like legumes and nuts. They add variety and nutritional richness to your protein-packed meals.

Flexible Eating

- **Diverse choices:** Enjoy a wide range of foods from different food groups. This includes a mix of proteins, carbohydrates, fruits, vegetables, and healthy fats.

- **Moderation mindset:** Practice moderation and portion control. Allow yourself the flexibility to indulge in treats while maintaining a foundation of nutritious choices.

- **Listen to your body:** Pay attention to your body's cues. Include a particular food in your meal plan if it makes you feel good. If not, explore alternative options.

Meal planning is a personalized adventure, and your preferences play a central role. Whether you follow a specific dietary path or enjoy a mix of culinary delights, the key is to nourish your body with wholesome, enjoyable meals.

Budget-Friendly Cooking

Embrace the power of versatile and cost-effective ingredients. Beans, lentils, rice, and pasta are pantry staples and the foundation for many delicious and budget-friendly meals. Explore the world of affordable yet nutritious options to elevate your culinary creations.

Unlock the secret to significant savings by purchasing staples in bulk. Items like grains, legumes, and spices are often more affordable when bought in larger quantities, reducing costs.

Transform leftovers into new meals. Cooked vegetables can find new life in a hearty soup and yesterday's roasted chicken into a flavorful stir-fry. The key is to view leftovers as opportunities for creativity rather than mere remnants.

Let the seasons guide your menu. Opt for seasonal produce, which tends to be more affordable and fresh at its peak. Visit local farmers' markets for budget-friendly and flavorful options supporting your wallet and local growers.

Take control of your kitchen by making essential items at home. From sauces and dressings to spice blends, creating these staples allows you to tailor flavors to your liking and often proves more economical than store-bought alternatives.

Smart Shopping Quest—Making Informed Grocery Choices

Learn the art of picking ingredients like a pro, making choices that are good for your meals, and contributing to a sustainable planet.

Arm yourself with a well-thought-out meal plan and a comprehensive shopping list. This strategic approach helps you stay focused, avoid impulse purchases, and save money by purchasing only what you need.

Navigate the aisles with a keen eye for price comparisons. Whether checking unit prices or opting for generic and store brands, a mindful approach to comparing prices ensures you get the best value for your money.

Transform your shopping experience by watching for discounts, sales, and promotions. Buying in bulk during sales provides immediate savings and contributes to long-term budget efficiency.

While meat can be pricier, consider incorporating more budget-friendly plant-based proteins into your meals. When choosing meat, choose less expensive cuts or explore bulk options to freeze portions for later use.

Strike a balance between new and frozen produce. While fresh is fantastic, don't underestimate the value of frozen fruits and vegetables. They often cost less, have a longer shelf life, and retain their nutritional value, offering budget-friendly alternatives.

Connect with your community and make conscious choices by supporting local farmers and exploring seasonal produce. This fosters a sense of community and presents budget-friendly and environmentally-conscious options.

Champion the cause of waste reduction by buying only what you need and finding creative ways to use leftovers. Freeze perishable items before they expire to minimize food waste and stretch your budget further.

Conclusion

Recap of Essential Life Skills

- **Communication skills:** Your voice is a powerful instrument, and you've mastered the art of communication. Whether expressing your thoughts or empathetically listening to others, you understand the profound impact of words.

- **Time management:** The clock is not an adversary but a companion on your journey. You've learned to navigate time purposefully, making each moment count and creating a life rich with experiences.

- **Emotional intelligence:** The landscape of emotions is no longer uncharted territory. You've cultivated emotional intelligence, fostering a deep understanding of yourself and others. Empathy is now your guiding compass.

- **Goal setting and planning:** Dreams are no longer distant stars but destinations on your roadmap. From short-term objectives to ambitious long-term goals, you've become a skilled architect of your future.

- **The basics of personal finance:** Money is a tool, and you've learned to wield it wisely. The fundamentals of personal finance are at your fingertips, setting the stage for financial empowerment.

- **Problem-solving and critical thinking:** Challenges are not barriers but gateways to growth. Equipped with problem-solving and critical thinking skills, you face obstacles with creativity, turning setbacks into stepping stones.

- **Making friends and building relationships:** Your social skills are finely tuned, creating connections. Making friends and nurturing relationships has become an art, enriching your life with shared experiences.

- **Health and well-being:** Your body and mind are sacred spaces, and you've embraced practices that honor them. You've laid the foundation for a flourishing life, from proper exercise to quality sleep, nourishing nutrition, and effective stress management.

- **Adaptability and resilience:** Life is a dynamic journey; you've become its adept navigator. Your adaptability and resilience ensure you weather storms and emerge stronger from them.

- **Cooking skills:** The kitchen is your canvas, and you've painted it with culinary mastery. From essential tools to cooking techniques, you've become an artist in the kitchen.

Encouragement for Continued Growth and Development

Let these words encourage you as you turn the page to the next chapter of your life.

Stay curious! The world is a vast playground of knowledge and experiences. Cultivate a spirit of curiosity, and let it lead you into uncharted territories.

Embrace every challenge! Challenges are not roadblocks but invitations to grow. Embrace them as opportunities for learning and personal transformation.

Celebrate all your successes! Take a moment to bask in the glow of your achievements, no matter how small. Each success is a testament to your capabilities and resilience.

Always try to connect with others. Life is a shared journey. Foster connections with diverse souls, listen to their stories, and build a community that uplifts and supports one another.

Continue to set new goals for yourself. Your journey of growth is ongoing. Dream bigger dreams, and continue planning for the extraordinary future that awaits.

Remember, your journey does not conclude here; it evolves. Every day is an opportunity for growth, and every experience is a stepping stone to the person you are becoming. The skills you've acquired are not just tools; they are companions on this exhilarating adventure called life.

As you step into the world with confidence, curiosity, and a heart brimming with resilience, remember that the best is yet to come. You are not merely equipped for the journey; you are destined for greatness. The world awaits the unique contributions that only you can make. So go forth, brave soul, and let your journey be a testament to your boundless potential. Your story is still unfolding and promises to be nothing short of extraordinary. Happy continued growth and development!

HELP SOMEONE ELSE BY PAYING IT FORWARD

Hello Fantastic Readers!

Hope you've enjoyed this book! We wanted to have a quick chat about something pretty cool that you can do – something that not only adds positively to your own experience but also pays it forward to others.

"Remember, there's no such thing as a small act of kindness. Every act creates a ripple with no logical end." - Scott Adams

Recently, we stumbled upon this amazing book called "Life Skills for Teens Made Simple." Trust us, it's a real game-changer! Now, we know life keeps you busy, but hang tight because this is genuinely worth your attention!

Have you ever thought about the impact you could have on someone else's life just by sharing your experience? We're not talking about changing the world overnight, but we are talking about contributing to someone's journey in a meaningful way.

Here's a quick question – have you ever come across a book or resource that genuinely made a difference in your life? Of course you have! Now imagine if someone took a moment to share that valuable find with you. It's like passing on a torch of knowledge and making the path a bit brighter for everyone.

So, here's the deal – leaving a review for "Life Skills for Teens Made Simple" is your chance to pay it forward. By sharing your thoughts, you're creating a roadmap for someone who might be navigating the challenges of teenage life.

Now, we understand if you're wondering, "Why should I take the time to leave a review?" Well, here's the scoop. Your review can help others decide if this book is the right fit for them. You become a friendly guide helping someone find the right path.

So, we're throwing out a friendly ask – can you spare a few minutes to leave an honest review for "Life Skills for Teens Made Simple"? Trust us; it's a small action that can make a big impact.

Just scan this QR Code or click this link: It's easy as pie!

https://www.amazon.com/review/create-review/?ie=UTF8&channel=glance-detail&asin=1963697006

Now, picture the ripple effect – your words can inspire, motivate, direct, and uplift others by passing a good deed that creates an amazing chain reaction. Plus, it feels pretty satisfying to know you're helping others, right? Think about the joy of knowing you've paid it forward by introducing something valuable to someone else. You're not just leaving a review; you're sharing your insight and making a positive impact.

So, what do you say, awesome reader? Let's pay it forward together and help others discover the greatness of "Life Skills for Teens Made Simple." Your review might be just the encouragement someone needs!

With much gratitude,

Arm In Arm Publishing Team

References

Abraham, N. (2019, July 22). *Can one embrace change? And is this an important lesson to teach young people?* Age of Awareness. https://medium.com/age-of-awareness/can-we-teach-students-how-to-embrace-change-4abeac2f058f

Ahuja, N. (2023, October 1). *Mastering self-care: your path to resilience and clarity.* Psychology Today. https://www.psychologytoday.com/us/blog/striving-high/202310/mastering-self-care-your-path-to-resilience-and-clarity

Ambre, D. (2020, September 23). *Three small-but-mighty phrases to empower your teen.* Ambre Associates. https://www.ambreassociates.com/blog/3-small-but-mighty-phrases-to-empower-your-teen

American Academy of Child and Adolescent Psychiatry. (2017, September). *Teen brain: behavior, problem-solving, and decision making.* American Academy of Child and Adolescent Psychiatry. https://www.aacap.org/aacap/families_and_youth/facts_for_families/fff-guide/the-teen-brain-behavior-problem-solving-and-decision-making-095.aspx

Berg, M. H. (2016, November 29). *Want your teen to be able to get a job? Make sure they have these skills.* Your Teen Magazine. https://yourteenmag.com/teens-college/college-life/soft-skills-for-teens

BetterHelp Editorial Team. (2021, August 25). *Coping skills for teens: how to handle difficult emotions.* Better Help.

https://www.betterhelp.com/advice/teenagers/coping-skills-for-teens-how-to-handle-difficult-emotions/

Black Press Media. (2023, March 22). *Raising resilient teens: tips for building adaptability skills*. The Ashcroft-Cache Creek Journal. https://www.ashcroftcachecreekjournal.com/community/raising-resilient-teens-tips-for-building-adaptability-skills-5882214

Boys & Girls Clubs of America. (2022, January 19). *The importance of goal-setting for teens*. Bgca.org. https://bgca.org/news-stories/2022/January/the-importance-of-goal-setting-for-teens?gad_source=1&gclid=Cj0KCQiA1rSsBhDHARIsANB4EJY1qTOyHr-4xcuqwXPYimCCZy7HBC-bnE2NO4BXG-IEIdlGa9NTO7saAvxSEALw_wcB

Bunyan, A. (2022, December 19). *How to set the best goals for you in the new year!* Common Threads. https://www.commonthreads.org/blog/goal-setting/?gclid=Cj0KCQiA1rSsBhDHARIsANB4EJYGhZ0EpfSQM1kiFidvvWvY9DQ1kWuQzJzgbMUAFKaFfk_uZ_3bpZcaAi5lEALw_wcB

Chowdhury, M. R. (2019, January 22). *What is emotional resilience and how to build it? (+Training Exercises)*. Positive Psychology. https://positivepsychology.com/emotional-resilience/

Ciranka, S., & van den Bos, W. (2019). Social influence in adolescent decision-making: a formal framework. *Frontiers in Psychology, 10*. https://doi.org/10.3389/fpsyg.2019.01915

Crevin, M. (2020, July 14). *Listen more, talk less and other tips for better communication*. Your Teen Magazine.

https://yourteenmag.com/family-life/communication/ways-to-improve-communication

Dawson, P. (2021). Helping children and teens strengthen executive skills to reach their full potential. *Archives of Clinical Neuropsychology*, *36*(7), 1279–1282. https://doi.org/10.1093/arclin/acab057

Dekin, S. (2020, April 17). *Why teenagers need to start discussing their emotions*. Mission Harbor Behavioral Health. https://sbtreatment.com/blog/teenagers-discussing-emotions/

Dolin, A. (2022, November 29). *Time management for teens: 10 tips for tackling schoolwork*. Ectutoring.com. https://ectutoring.com/time-management-for-teens

Getz, L. (2022, November 10). *Change can be scary for kids but here's how parents can help them embrace it*. Parents. https://www.parents.com/change-can-be-scary-for-kids-but-here-s-how-parents-can-help-them-embrace-it-6752500

Ginsburg, K. (2018a, September 4). *Ensuring strong connections for teens*. Center for Parent and Teen Communication. https://parentandteen.com/building-strong-connections-for-teens-and-families/

Ginsburg, K. (2018b, September 4). *Support teens to release emotions*. Center for Parent and Teen Communication. https://parentandteen.com/support-teens-release-emotions/

Hale, L. (2008, April 29). *Embracing change: adolescence to adulthood*. Dr. Liz Hale. https://drlizhale.com/embracing-change-adolescence-to-adulthood/

Hall, S. L. (2019, November 4). *She said what?! How to help teens when they're frustrated with a friend.* Your Teen Magazine. https://yourteenmag.com/social-life/teenagers-friends/how-to-avoid-misunderstandings

Holbrook, S. (2017, July 27). *Helping our kids learn how to speak up.* Your Teen Magazine. https://yourteenmag.com/family-life/communication/speak-for-themselves

Introducing the Eisenhower matrix. (2011). Eisenhower. https://www.eisenhower.me/eisenhower-matrix/

Kirk, V. (2022, December 2). *Teaching adaptability to help students succeed.* Connections Academy. https://www.connectionsacademy.com/support/resources/article/teaching-adaptability-helps-students-succeed/

Kovacs, S. (2020, January 2). *#ThoughtfulThursday: teenage EQ and adaptability.* Ambassador Leaders. https://ambassadorleaders.com/toolkit/eq-adaptability

Kukulus, J. (2015, March 10). *The art of saying no.* Adolescent Counseling Services. https://www.acs-teens.org/the-art-of-saying-no/#:~:text=For%20teens%20who%20have%20a

Listen up: how active listening unlocks a growth mindset for teens. (2023, October 21) College MatchPoint. https://www.collegematchpoint.com/listen-up-how-active-listening-unlocks-a-growth-mindset-for-teens

Mastering effective communication skills in high school: a social emotional learning journey. Everyday Speech. (2023, August 7). Everyday Speech. https://everydayspeech.com/sel-implementation/mastering-effective-communication-skills-in-high-school-a-social-emotional-learning-journey/

Mental Health America. (2023). *What is emotional intelligence and how does it apply to the workplace?* Mental Health America. https://mhanational.org/what-emotional-intelligence-and-how-does-it-apply-workplace#:~:text=Emotional%20Intelligence%20(EI)%20is%20the

Morin, A. (2019). *Steps to teaching your teen how to make good decisions.* Verywell Family. https://www.verywellfamily.com/steps-to-good-decision-making-skills-for-teens-2609104

Nemours Kids Health. (2021, January 29). *Understanding your emotions (for teens).* Nemours Kids Health. https://kidshealth.org/en/teens/understand-emotions.html

Neuroscience News. (2022, October 30). *Teenage brains: what is happening and why it leads to more risky behaviors.* Neuroscience News. https://neurosciencenews.com/teenage-brains-risk-21757/

Newport Academy Staff. (2020, August 17). *Empowering teens: talking about the do's instead of the don'ts.* Newport Academy. https://www.newportacademy.com/resources/empowering-teens/empowering-teens/

Office of Population Affairs. (n.d.-a). *Healthy behavior.* Opa.hhs.gov. https://opa.hhs.gov/adolescent-health/physical-health-developing-adolescents/healthy-behavior

Office of Population Affairs. (n.d.-b). *Physical health in developing adolescents.* Opa.hhs.gov. https://opa.hhs.gov/adolescent-health/physical-health-developing-adolescents

Office of Population Affairs. (2022). *Healthy relationships in adolescence.* Opa.hhs.gov. https://opa.hhs.gov/adolescent-health/healthy-relationships-adolescence

Pfeiffer, J. W. (1998). Conditions that hinder effective communication. *The Pfeiffer Library*, 6. https://home.snu.edu/~jsmith/library/body/v06.pdf

Queensland Government. (2020, September 2). *How to help teenagers make good decisions.* Spark Their Future. https://www.sparktheirfuture.qld.edu.au/how-to-help-your-teen-make-good-decisions-about-school-and-life/

Coping skills, resilience and teenagers. (n.d.).Reach Out Parent. https://parents.au.reachout.com/skills-to-build/wellbeing/coping-skills-resilience-and-teenagers#:~:text=

Roehlkepartain, E., Pekel, K., Syvertsen, A., Sethi, J., Sullivan, T., & Scales, P. (2017). *Creating connections that help young people thrive relationships first.* https://sites.ed.gov/nsaesc/files/2017/07/12758351-0-FINALRelationships-F1.pdf

Russell, L. (2023, September 25). *Goal setting for teens: the SMART way to success {parent guide}.* They Are the Future. https://www.theyarethefuture.co.uk/smart-goals-teens/#:~:text=Here%20are%20some%20ideas%20for

Smith, K. (2022, October 21). *Six common triggers of teen stress.* Psycom. https://www.psycom.net/common-triggers-teen-stress

Sosnoski, K. (2021, October 4). *Why (and how!) to foster self-expression healthily.* Psych Central. https://psychcentral.com/blog/a-mini-guide-for-expressing-yourself-effectively-with-anyone

Sweet, J. (2018, June 18). *Attentive listening helps teens share their challenges, study finds.* Verywell Mind. https://www.verywellmind.com/attentive-listening-helps-teens-share-their-challenges-5189401

Tomás-Keegan, M. (2020, February 25). *Resiliency in the face of adversity: Six ways to become more resilient.* Transition & Thrive with María. https://transitionandthrivewithmaria.com/resiliency-in-the-face-of-adversity-6-ways-become-more-resilient/

United Way NCA. (2023, June 6). *Youth financial literacy: why is it important?* United Way NCA. https://unitedwaynca.org/blog/financial-literacy-for-youth/

University College London. (2023, May 31). *Nurturing healthy friendships: the key to mental well-being.* Global Business School for Health. https://www.ucl.ac.uk/global-business-school-health/news/2023/may/nurturing-healthy-friendships-key-mental-well-being-0

University of Rochester Medical Center. (n.d.). *Exercise and teenagers.* Www.urmc.rochester.edu. https://www.urmc.rochester.edu/encyclopedia/content.aspx?ContentTypeID=90&ContentID=P01602#:~:text=Physical%20activity%20should%20include%20aerobic

Vaccaro, P. J. (2000). The 80/20 rule of time management. *Family Practice Management,* 7(8), 76–76. https://www.aafp.org/pubs/fpm/issues/2000/0900/p76.html#:~:text=Simply%20put%2C%20the%2080%2F20

Vallejo, M. (2023, October 6) *Time management for teens: challenges, strategies, and tips.* Mental Health Center Kids.

https://mentalhealthcenterkids.com/blogs/articles/time-management-for-teens

Welker, E. (2010, April 23). *Decision making/problem solving with teens*. Ohioline Ohio State University Extension. https://ohioline.osu.edu/factsheet/HYG-5301

Why exercise is wise (for teens). (2018, February). Nemours Ten Health. https://kidshealth.org/en/teens/exercise-wise.html

Made in the USA
Las Vegas, NV
23 April 2024